Kenny Blue

The
Beach House

An Urban Tale of Envy, Lust, Lies and Betrayal

*J*ourney **Publishing**

Library of Congress Control Number: 2004111374

ISBN 0-9760295-0-2

First Printing (Collector's Edition) 2005

For information regarding book club or bulk purchase discounts, please contact Journey Publishing through one of the following methods:

Phone: 678-464-1882
journeypublish@bellsouth.net
PMB 145, 8200 Mall Parkway, Suite 135
Lithonia, GA 30058

Journey
Publishing

Printed in the U.S.A. by
Morris Publishing
3212 East Highway 30
Kearney, NE 68847
1-800-650-7888

Dedication

This book is dedicated to Curtis Dee Tucker, AKA "Lil' Tick."
Sunrise: September 26, 1939—Sunset: July 16, 1992.
May your spirit and legacy live on. I'll see you on the other side.

Kenny

Acknowledgements

Before I thank anyone for supporting and encouraging me throughout the creation of this project, I must first thank God for answering my prayers. It would be difficult to describe how I felt that morning, because the vision you provided me was so clear and beautiful it was scary. I don't know where this is headed, but I'm ready for the ride. I love you. Thank you.

Okay, now to the folks who have been there from the beginning, and saw this thing through to the end. "Momma Lea," where do I start? You always told me you saw a sparkle in my eyes when I was born. It would be a pleasure for me to show you how my determination and persistence unravels before your eyes. I hope you are proud. Thanks for the financial aid... Oh yeah, buy something nice with that interest. I love you! To my lovely wife and beautiful daughter, thank you for displaying patience with all of my late night sessions on the computer. You thought I was chatting with some woman, huh? Tell the truth (LOL). Totty Jones, my homegirl, the superwoman of the decade, thank you for being real with the constructive criticism, and showing me what true faith is. Remember that day at the sushi restaurant? Thanks for being my bootleg editor: not bad for a rookie! Kelly, the same goes for you. Thanks for utilizing that Language Arts degree, double-checking my manuscript, and telling it like it is. True friends are hard to find.

Uncle Kenny, you have been there for me as a father figure for many years and I can't thank you enough for that. Your constant encouragement for my many ideas and endeavors has helped me reach this point in my life. It really is amazing to wake up each morning to something you love to do each and every day.

To my "mentor," Electa Rome-Parks, thank you so much for schooling me on the business of selling and marketing books. It truly has been a blessing to have such an ambitious, determined, and encouraging person in my corner on those days where I wanted to throw the towel in. Congratulations on your new deal; I wish you the greatest success. Marissa, thanks for giving me further insight into the self-publishing business. I wish you continued success on your third release, *Hot Boyz*. To Brandi and Trent at B's Books and More: thank you for supporting my efforts, and checking on me at the house parties :). I look forward to working with you guys real soon. Kevin, AKA "Kaiwen," thanks for asking me every month if the manuscript was done. You are going to get the very first copy, I promise! Thanks for hooking up the website too (you computer whizzes kill me; you make it look so easy!). Stacey, your tea functions are the bomb! I was so scared the first time I almost boo-booed on myself. I was shocked when I read that chapter and received a standing ovation. We must do that again real soon. To the many websites that provided vital research information for this project, thank you too. Finally, I MUST thank my computer for putting up with my finger hacking for eight long months. Wow, I might treat you to an upgrade. If I forgot anybody, please forgive me. I got your back next go round.

—Kenny Blue

Temptation rarely comes in working hours.
It is in their leisure hours that men are
made or marred.

                    - W.M. Taylor

Prologue

Monday Morning, Lithonia Georgia, 7:20 am

The heavy volume of Monday morning rush-hour traffic on I-20 was reaching its peak. Felicia alternated her attention between the vanity mirror on her car's sun visor and the crazies that were attempting to use the emergency lane of the highway's right shoulder as a way to skate past the stop-and-go parade of semi's, SUV's, tow trucks, and passenger cars that blocked all three lanes of the debris-ridden highway. *Wow,* Felicia thought, *this is amazing. Every time I call myself leaving on time, I end up running into this doggone traffic. Where are all these people coming from?*

As she continued to play with her half-done hair and apply some cheap mascara from Dollar General that she kept in the glove compartment for insurance, the blaring, incessant sound of car horns began to rattle her nerves. She powered on her car radio, and pressed the seek button until she reached KISS 104.1 FM. She tuned in just in time to hear the news segment of the *Tom Joyner Morning Show*, the regular highlight of her daily morning commute. As she approached the Wesley Chapel exit, the traffic became a parking lot, as drivers craned their necks to witness the fate of one of the crazies who had been pulled over by a DeKalb County police officer in a charcoal gray cruiser with black and gold lettering and black wall tires. As she slowly crept past the embarrassed law-breaker, she flipped her sun visor back into its proper position and increased the volume on her radio. A light wind gust lapped at her late-model silver Toyota Camry, causing it to sway quietly in the early May sunrise, while she awaited her passage to freedom at the interchange of I-20 and I-285. She focused her attention on the radio conversation, which had strayed from a news story about a cross-dressing bank bandit in Arizona to what passengers were going to be wearing on the upcoming *Fantastic Voyage* cruise.

"Speaking of dress," Tom quipped. "I wonder how many big women are gonna try to wear a bikini during the cruise?"

"Aww, Tom," Sybil said.

"Oh boy," Miss Dupree added, with a thick Cajun accent. Jay Anthony Brown was acting comedic as usual, as he responded to Tom's general question.

"Playa," Jay started, "I don't know how many big women are going to try that on the cruise THIS year, but I gotta tell ya; playa, when we were on the beach for the water-gun fight LAST year, I saw Ms. Wide-Load Wallace wearin' a tight black two-piece bikini, black goggles with a shark hologram on 'em, and a extra-small life vest."

Laughter erupted, as Sybil's high-pitched giggle escalated into a cry for Jay's mercy.

"Huh, huh, huh, huh, huh... Jay, stop!" Sybil begged, as she convulsed in anticipation for his punch line. Tom and Miss Dupree doubled over in laughter.

"What was she doing, player?" Tom asked, as he tried to control the laughter that caused tears to roll down his cheeks.

"Playa," Jay said, sounding serious yet somber, "she eeaassed into the water, took a deep breath, and disappeared under the waves."

"Then what, player?" Tom asked, barely able to contain himself. "People slooowly began to disappear, one-by-one, while we ran around on the beach squirtin' each other up." Jay flashed a pearly smile at his co-workers, as Felicia giggled from the confines of her car's cockpit.

"Whhat?" Sybil said, as she snickered uncontrollably.

"Yeah, Sybil, you didn't notice all that unclaimed baggage when we got back to Miami?" Jay said. The musical cue to go to commercial elevated in volume, as the radio personalities laughed heartily in the background.

Boy, they sound like they're having a good time, Felicia thought. Her melancholy mood had just been broken. She was determined not to allow the devil beat her down this Monday morning. She cleared the nasty traffic jam, mashed the accelerator, and sailed towards Sandy Springs on I-285.

Twenty-three minutes later, Felicia was making a right onto Ashford-Dunwoody Road, zooming through two yellow lights towards the ultra-modern office complex that housed Concepts Marketing. She trounced over several speed bumps, entered the employee garage, and parked on the second level near the covered walkway. She checked her half-made face one last time, brushed some waffle crumbs off of her navy blue Sag Harbor pantsuit, grabbed her black leather briefcase from the backseat, and took the familiar stroll towards the building's atrium.

Felicia entered the thirty-story complex, and walked towards the security desk. She spoke to Sam, whom she and her fellow marketing consultants referred to affectionately as "Sam the Security Guard."

"Good morning, Sam," Felicia said playfully, looking for one of his trademark replies. Sam flashed a sleepy smile, as he watched Felicia scan her security badge.

"Good morning for YOU," Sam said, in his usual smart-alecky tone of voice. "Shoot, I've been here since twelve midnight, and I've got one hour to go; ain't nuthin moved up in here 'cept the rats, cats, and my Little Debbies," he said while leaning back in his black leather chair and scratching his pot belly through his uniform. White stubble and wrinkled age lines adorned his chin and face, displaying years of underpaid, menial labor. His dark complexion, chiseled cheeks, and wide nose, however, painted a different story. It showed a unique proudness, a defiance of economic hardship, and a lineage that could only be traced back to a proud continent of African kings, hunters, tradesmen, artisans, and warriors. An empty red and yellow box of Golden Cremes peeked innocently out of the black wastebasket on Sam's left side. His small clock radio played an old Sam Cooke cut called "A Change Is Gonna Come," as Felicia chuckled at his comment.

"You want some coffee Sam?" she asked, trying to perk him up as usual, before his shift ended.

"You know what, Mrs. Sampson? I believe I will. God is gonna bless you, watch what I tell ya."

"Thanks Sam," Felicia said, as she made her way past the security desk towards the snack shop to purchase two cups of Seattle's Best coffee. After making Sam's coffee, and topping her cup of coffee off with vanilla cappuccino, Felicia headed towards the cash register to pay.

"Sleepy this morning, huh?" the polite female clerk said. Her youthful smile and mocha-toned skin matched her shapely figure perfectly. Her large, brown eyes sparkled with enthusiasm.

"I'm beginning to wake up now, but this cup is going to Sam, the security guard. Would you mind making sure it gets to him, sweetheart? I'm running a few minutes late."

"Not a problem. That'll be two sixty-eight." She slung her beaded cornrows to the side, and extended her neatly manicured hand. Felicia paid up, grabbed her coffee, and hustled towards the elevators. She joined a few of her co-workers, as well as employees from other companies housed in the building, and exited on the twenty-fifth floor. She greeted Allison, the receptionist, and continued down the hallway past the noisy call-center towards her semi-private tan cubicle, a small space that she called home from eight to five. She spoke to Antoine Jones, her cubicle neighbor, and Greg Hall, another neighbor who made his workdays move faster by sending e-mail jokes around the office. She sat her briefcase and coffee down, rolled her black leather high back chair away from her desk, and sat down. She powered on her computer, and proceeded to check her e-mail.

The first few messages were Spam. *Fast Credit Repair. Delete. Own Timeshares Worldwide. Delete. Find Your Classmates Online. Delete. Auto Reply: Out of the Office. Delete. MBA 8240 Final Exam Schedule.* Felicia clicked the mouse to read the message.

The final exam for Strategic Marketing Techniques will be held next Tuesday in the RCB building, room 203 from 6-8 pm.

Any student unable to attend is required to call my graduate assistant and schedule a proctored exam to be taken this Thursday.

Best Regards,

Dr. Shockley

Felicia suddenly felt like she was on the verge of having an anxiety attack. She saved the message in her Georgia State folder, and let out a deep breath. *God, when will this end? I feel overwhelmed. I'm trying to study for school, be a mom, AND keep up with my clients. If I earn a B in this class, my GPA will drop below a 3.5. Lord, please help me through this! After this is over, I promise to be the best mom and wife I can possibly be.* Just as Felicia ended her thoughts, her phone rang.

Logan Reed? I wonder what this can be about? It's not even 8:30.

Felicia pushed the blinking extension button, and picked up the receiver.

"Good morning Felicia, it's Logan."

"Good morning Logan; happy Monday."

"Felicia, listen. I need for you to be in my office at 10:00 sharp. I have something very important to discuss with you. Kym Kersey will be there as well."

"Okay, I'll be there."

"Sounds good. See you then." Logan hung up the phone, while Felicia sat in silence with the receiver still glued to her ear. She was trying to figure out why Logan would want to see her, and why Kym was invited. *Is this what I think it is?* Felicia asked herself. Rumors had been circulating about a downsizing for months, and associates with the smallest client portfolio were going to be the first to go. Although Felicia knew her portfolio was not the smallest, it was possible that some of her clients may have complained to upper-management about the attention their marketing plans were getting. Felicia's mind began to race. *Severance Package, Mortgage, Jordan's Private School Tuition.*

Felicia suddenly remembered that Jordan needed to be picked up from school. She had a study group meeting at Georgia State after work, and wouldn't make it home until after 8:30. She kept the receiver on her ear, found a free extension, and called her husband Kelvin on his cell.

"Hello!" Kelvin yelled, over the scream of heavy machinery.

"Kelvin, it's me," Felicia said, trying to keep her voice level to a minimum.

"Hold on," Kelvin replied, as he walked towards a quiet office in the Ford Assembly Plant.

"Alright; what's up?"

"Kelvin, can you pick Jordan up from school today? I have a study group meeting today that I forgot to tell you about."

"Yeah, no problem. Just make sure you try to remember next time. I was supposed to go shoot some pool and watch the playoffs with Mack and the boys."

"Okay Kelvin. Just remember, you DO have some family obligations."

"Yeah, so do you. Anyway, let me get off this phone before I lose a car on this line. I'll holla at 'chu later."

"You do that." The frustrated couple disconnected their conversation and eased back into their daily routines.

*　　*　　*

Felicia glanced at the silver digital clock radio that sat next to her computer. The time read 8:52. Her e-mail was still up, so she deleted two more messages, and opened the last one that was named *GEORGE CARLIN STRIKES AGAIN* sent by Greg.

1. If 4 out of 5 people SUFFER from diarrhea...does that mean that one enjoys it?

2. There are three religious truths:

a) *Jews do not recognize Jesus as the Messiah*
b) *Protestants do not recognize the Pope as the leader of the Christian faith*
c) *Baptists do not recognize each other in the liquor store or at Hooters.*

3. If it's true that we are here to help others, then what exactly are the others here for?

Felicia's mood had once again been lifted. If it wasn't for those early morning laughs, Felicia wondered how she would be able to make it. Just as she began to catch up on the files of some of her clients, Antoine popped into her cubicle.

"Knock, knock," he said, trying not to startle her.

"Good morning Antoine," Felicia said, as she turned to face her co-worker. She scanned his youthful, clean-shaven face. His skin was a golden-bronze, and his short hair cut was accentuated with a thin beard line that connected both ears. His piercing hazel brown eyes and perfect white teeth were fixed for her attention. A peach colored Gitman Brothers button down shirt and neatly pressed khaki dress pants draped his six-foot frame. A pair of tan Mocc Oxfords completed the ensemble, giving the impression that Antoine wasn't hurting for money.

"Felicia, we need to talk."

"About what?" Felicia replied.

"Me and Shauna. She's afraid about the moving into my house before we get married situation."

"I should've figured. Antoine, you're going to get it together sooner or later, and it needs to be sooner than later."

"I know, Felicia, but it's hard when you've never been through this before. Can we talk about it again over lunch? My treat."

"Yes, Antoine, I guess we can. Listen, have you heard anything new about those downsizing rumors?"

"No, not since a couple of weeks ago. That's the last thing on my mind right now. Why, what's up?"

"Nothing...I was just asking, that's all."

Just then, Felicia's phone rang. It looked like one of her clients. She excused herself and went back to work. She completed a round of phone calls, responded to a few old e-mails, and checked her task list on her Outlook program. She logged off at 9:50 and headed towards Logan's office for their meeting. She walked past the break room, peeking her head in to speak to Stacey Larieux, an attractive young graduate of Clark-Atlanta, and Damien Harris, a newly hired employee from Charlotte. She knocked on Logan's door, and was invited in. Kym was already there, and Logan was sitting in a plush, black leather chair tapping a Pilot Rollerball pen nervously on the mahogany desk.

"Am I late?" Felicia asked, checking her wristwatch. It read 9:57.

"No, you're right on time," Logan said. "Have a seat. Listen, I know you two are busy, so I'm going to get right to it. I have a project that could boost not only your careers, but the status of Concepts as well."

Felicia exhaled sharply, as a wave of relief swept through her inner-core. *Thank God,* she thought. *I thought I was going to be told to clean my cubicle out.*

"There's only one catch, though. I felt I needed to run it by you first."

"Okay," Felicia said. She glanced at Kym, who looked puzzled.

"First of all, you all are going to have to collaborate as a team. I know that's rare for you, and you all have individual accounts, so we're going to have to transfer some of them to other associates in your absence."

"In our absence?" Kym asked.

"Yes. Two weeks ago, I spoke with a representative from the Atlanta Convention and Visitor's Bureau. They want to outsource their marketing plan for the first time. With the fiscal problems affecting the city's budget, especially the sewer overhaul, they are desperately trying to find ways to increase business and tourism in Atlanta. I submitted the winning bid, and have selected you two to lead the team."

"Thanks, Logan," Felicia said.

"So what's the catch?" Kym said.

"The catch is, I want the team to be African-American."

"Excuse me?" Felicia said.

"You heard me right. The only specification in the bid regarding the winning contractor was that the team be made up of African-Americans only. Apparently, some civil-rights groups and politicians have been complaining about the lack of diversity on the bureau's website and in their business practices. An investigative review concluded that the City of Atlanta has lost millions of dollars in potential revenue, and suffered from negative publicity. The bureau wants to be proactive by recovering that revenue and improving minority relations. So it's up to you two to make that happen."

"Wow. That sounds like a spoonful," Kym said.

"It is. Now here's the other part. The first draft is to be completed within the next two weeks, which is breakneck speed for a marketing plan of this caliber. So this weekend, while you all enjoyed your free time, I made phone calls to contacts and friends around the country to see if anyone had a timeshare or anything so you guys could work in seclusion. I got lucky. One of my contacts has a timeshare at St. George Island, down in Florida. It's near Panama City Beach, about a six or seven hour drive from here. I figured you guys could use this week to catch up on your clients, inform them of the transfers, and be ready to leave by next Thursday."

"This is a lot to absorb, Logan," Felicia said.

"I know. That's why I'm giving you the next week and a half to get yourselves together. I need the best marketing plan you've ever done in your lives. It would mean a lot to me. By the way, here is a list of people that I put together. This is your team. Get to know them if you don't already."

Logan handed Felicia and Kym the list that was scribbled on a sheet of paper printed with company letterhead. They browsed over the list, examining each name carefully. Leslie Battle. Antoine Jones. Damien Harris. Stacey Larieux. Kym Kersey. Felicia Sampson. They both made mental notes, and excused themselves for a hectic day of re-scheduling.

*   *   *

1 Friday Morning

The sun's morning rays were just beginning to peek through the pine trees.

"Klummpt!" Damien was startled by the driver's side door of the red Taurus being slammed. After finding his bearings, he wiped the excess saliva from his chin, sat up, and looked around to see if anyone was watching him call the dogs.

Apparently, Stacey was just as tired. She was in the passenger seat in front of Damien, looking like she had been possessed by a gremlin. As she opened her eyes and regained her composure, she noticed Antoine and Leslie heading towards the door of the convenience store they had parked in front of. Damien told Stacey that he wanted to stretch, so she stepped out and let the passenger's seat up.

"Where are we?" Damien asked, trying to look sincere.

"I don't know," Stacey replied, taking a long stretch and yawn.

"You never answered my question," Damien said.

Stacey raised her voice to an irritated tone. "I just told you, I don't k—" Damien cut her off in mid-sentence. "I'm talking about the question I asked you back at Concepts in the break lounge last week. Do you have a man?" Damien put emphasis on his question, as if she owed him a response.

Stacey was offended. It was too early in the morning for anyone to be flirting, much less a co-worker that she barely knew. Last week, she had brushed Damien off with a smile. This time, she would have to bring out her Cajun mojo.

"Look, IF I have a man," Stacey responded, "It's none of your business." Her left hand was placed on her hip, which shifted for emphasis. Her right hand was close to Damien's face with a wagging forefinger attached. "Furthermore," she continued, "If I DON'T have a man, I definitely wouldn't have you as one. I already know your m.o."

Just as Stacey was about to continue reading her sly-grinning pursuer, Antoine emerged from the convenience store with a cold bottle of Yoo-Hoo, ready to pump a fresh tank of gas.

"Are you guys alright?" Antoine asked. His eyebrows rose with concern.

"Yeah, we're okay" Damien said, as he turned from Stacey's icy glare.

Stacey headed inside to join Leslie in the ladies room. She hoped that it was clean.

"Where are we?" Damien asked Antoine, this time in a serious tone.

"We're on the Georgia-Florida border, about to hit Tallahassee, home of my alma mater, FAAAMMMUUUU!"

Several of the store's redneck-looking customers stared in disgust, but Antoine didn't care. He had slept for four hours, and was excited about driving through the town that held the fond memories of his college experience. It also held a dark secret.

*   *   *

Felicia's cell phone rang. She opened her eyes reluctantly, and in her most groggy voice, greeted the caller.

"H-Hello?" her voice whispered.

"Felicia? Sorry to wake you lovebirds, but we need directions; this is Antoine."

"That's okay," Felicia responded, as she turned onto her back, struggling to clear the cobwebs that were clouding her thought process. "I thought you were from here," Felicia said, trying to steal a few extra seconds of beauty rest.

"I went to college down here," Antoine responded, "But I've never been to St. George, only Panama City and Daytona."

Felicia glanced at the small digital clock on the dresser. The numbers were fixed at 9:42 am. She adjusted her eyes, let out a big yawn, and stretched her free hand towards the ceiling.

God knows when I've had this much sleep, Felicia thought to herself. The quiet and solitude of the beach house was just what she needed to break her super-routine.

"Where are you?" Felicia continued, having to extend her antenna to keep from breaking up. "We just passed through Tallahassee. We're on 319 South."

Felicia gave Antoine the directions to the island, and hung up the phone. She rolled out of the soft queen bed that she shared with Kelvin, and went into the bathroom to relieve herself. She brushed her teeth, rinsed, and headed back to the bed to catch a few more dreams.

"Baby," Felicia said as she gently shook Kelvin's broad, muscular shoulders. No response. Again, she shook her husband's thick frame, this time, adding a kiss on the cheek.

"Aaaaw mann, what time is it?" Kelvin asked sincerely, not wanting to be the first human being conscious on the planet.

"It's almost ten o'clock. The rest of the crew will be here in a little while. Can you please go to the store and buy some food for us to cook?"

Felicia told Kelvin where to find the cash in her purse, and dozed back off into her dream wonderland.

After Kelvin gained his bearings, he duplicated Felicia's bathroom routine, and went to work with his electric shaver. He shaved the baby stubble from his face, toweled off, and walked over to the bedroom window, peeking through the horizontal mini-blinds to gauge the temperature outside. The sunlight was bright, causing his eyes to squint. After adjusting, he scanned a few beach houses that sat nearby. In the distance, he saw an elderly couple, two snowbirds walking in the morning sun. He also noticed a male jogger dressed in a white tank top, blue running shorts, and a yellow visor gliding effortlessly down a road that seemingly led to nowhere.

Kelvin slipped on some jean shorts, brown leather sandals, and a tan t-shirt with the numbers 770 stitched to the front. He went to his overnight bag, dabbed some cocoa butter into his palms, rubbed it on his arms and legs, and sprayed a small amount of cologne onto his body. He then grabbed the keys to his truck and headed towards the door to carry out his mission.

"What's up fool?" Kelvin was on his cell phone calling Ford, as if they couldn't survive for two days without him.

"Who's this, Kelvin?" the voice on the other end responded.

"Yeah, this is Kelvin. Look Mack," Kelvin said, changing his Decatur drawl to a serious tone. "Everything straight down there on the line?"

"Yeah, man," Mack replied, "But the boys down here miss you. We can't remember the last time you took off."

Mack's voice was barely audible over the scream of heavy machinery on the assembly line.

"How's the beach?" Mack asked. "You seen anything that could make it into Candies?"

"The beach is fine. I'm 'bout to check it out right now. We didn't get in until last night."

"Don't have too much fun. We wouldn't want to…" Mack's response became garble.

"We're breaking up," Kelvin said. "Just tell everybody I'm havin' a good time, and I'll tell your momma to call you when she wakes up." Mack let out a hysterical laugh, and said goodbye.

Kelvin was the kind of worker that a company like Ford coveted. Never late to work, always played team ball, and always made work fun for his employees. As long as his directions were followed, production was on par, and a smile was on your face, Kelvin was the ideal supervisor.

*   *   *

"Look at the signs!" Damien was demonstrative, as he simultaneously tapped Antoine's right shoulder and motioned towards the window. Antoine was trying to concentrate on the winding road, but peeked to the side long enough to observe the objects of Damien's curiosity. *You've got to be kidding; people in this part of Florida must not have much to do,* he thought. On what seemed like every fourth mailbox, was a sign that read "BAIT," with an arrow pointing towards a mixture of dilapidated trailers and depressed-looking homes. It seemed like every realty sign read either Folks or St. Joe. It was a monopoly over nothing, the type of real estate that you sell to a snowbird on speculation.

"That's crazy," Antoine responded, soaking in the fact that people could actually sleep with worms and minnows wiggling around in their living space. He tried to pretend that he was interested, but other things were weighing heavy on his mind. Like planning his Thanksgiving wedding, settling into his new home, and explaining to his fiancée's parents why she was selling her condo before their hook-up date. Love will do that to you, especially when you're due for a backslide. Antoine's mind was a racetrack. A thousand thoughts zoomed around in his subconscious, just like the number of bait signs he was passing trying to reach a company meeting on the beach. It was something he didn't look forward to doing, but something he knew he had to do.

Damien's thoughts were elsewhere too. He was just hired at Concepts Marketing three months ago. He never planned on taking a financial or professional step backwards, but then again, he had never been grown. At least that's what his momma always said. Charlotte, North Carolina was a bit different than Atlanta too. It was still Old South. Once you developed your reputation and gained your way into coveted social circles, your status changed. Your respect increased. Mutual associates encouraged and supported your ascent towards the peak of the corporate hierarchy instead of treating you with suspicion and disdain. In Atlanta, it was a survivor's game. He could tell the minute he stepped foot into Concepts. You were either part of the solution or you were out. Nothing personal. Just business. But Damien was a survivor. Always had been. Always would be. And nothing could change that.

In the back seat, Stacey and Leslie were sleeping so hard it looked like they were trying to trap horseflies in their mouths. The sudden change in routine must have been a shock to their anatomies. When they left Atlanta at four-something in the morning, everyone except Leslie was exhausted. Stacey didn't get much sleep after her open call modeling audition to promote Hennessey. She still had to pack, and packing for a diva was by no means easy. Leslie had probably gotten the most sleep out of the group prior to leaving, but she was hardly nocturnal. After four hours of night driving, she was beat. If she were to enjoy the sights on the Florida highways, it wouldn't be today.

"An IGA!" Damien sounded more excited than when he pointed the bait signs out to Antoine. "I haven't seen one of those since the shag was in!"

Antoine knew they were close to their destination, so he decided to be a more willing participant in acknowledging Damien's unimportant observations.

"It's probably the only grocery store in this town," Antoine responded.

"Yep." Damien's acknowledgement was accompanied by a smiling head nod.

"And they probably spent most of their advertising on that ugly-ass sign," Damien said, pointing a finger at the revolving red and white sign that invited shoppers into the parking lot.

Antoine agreed, but didn't speak. As a Christian, he was taught to display virtue over ignorance; and he was supposed to lead by example. But sometimes, it was difficult for him to let go of his old ways. And the tongue had always been his weapon of choice.

As Antoine navigated his fellow associates across a bridge leaving Carrabelle, his thoughts turned to Shauna. They had been together nearly every day for the past six months. They had even decided to shack, against their religious convictions. It felt strange not waking up in her arms. He coveted her presence. She was like a breath of fresh air. He worshipped her like a queen, just like granny and papa used to tell him. Because you never know which day could be your last. From the day he met her at their church's singles retreat, he knew she was the one. He was certain of it. And that brought a smile to his face, because up to this point in his life, uncertainty had been his bedmate. But that was about to change. He was sure of it.

*   *   *

Kelvin was excited. Before he got into the truck, he walked to the rear of the beach house and up the stairs leading to the deck. He wanted to steal a glimpse of Mother Nature's work. The view was spectacular. Just over the sand dunes, about one hundred yards past the termination point of the deck walkway, sat the largest, most incredible sight that Kelvin had seen in his life.

Growing up in Decatur was greater, as his "folk" from home would say, but this was amazing. The sounds of the ocean, the sight of countless waves, the morning songs created by brown and white seagulls a cappella style, and shimmering blue water as far as his eyes could see. The Gulf of Mexico was truly a sight to behold. Kelvin breathed as long and deep as he could. The air was thick and salty, but it was the cleanest air he had ever inhaled. It was the closest he had come to witnessing perfection, except the day Jordan came into the world. That was the most exciting day of his life. His first-born. A son. It was the first time he had recognized the true greatness of God. He had seen many amazing things in his lifetime, but that was truly a humbling experience. As Kelvin reminisced and admired the natural beauty surrounding him, he experienced a revelation. He knew immediately that he would have to step up his game as a father, and expose his son to more than he had seen growing up. He decided right then and there that he was going to take his daddy-husband routine to another level.

As Kelvin drove towards the island's convenience store, he noticed things that weren't there under the cover of darkness. Almost every house sat on stilts; at least that's what it looked like to him. A wide, asphalt pedestrian lane was smartly paved a few feet from the road, presumably to eliminate incidents of hit-and-runs. *Never would see that back home,* Kelvin thought to himself. Then he turned his attention to the approaching signs on the small number of businesses on the island. As he quickly glanced from left to right, he absorbed the names. St. George Resort Realty, Castaway Liquors, B.J.'s Pizza and Subs, St. George Island Bistro, and Gulf Coast Community Bank.

Next to the bistro was a man preparing to sell seafood from a trailer hooked to the back of a truck. Kelvin wondered if he could do the same before the Falcon's home games, and make a little change while he partied. Kelvin crossed a four-way intersection, and turned left onto Franklin Boulevard. The BP sign was approaching on his left. From the stares of the islands inhabitants, Kelvin assumed that the number of blacks in these parts was slim; especially the ones that drove Ford Expeditions with twenty-two inch chrome rims. He was riding with the windows down, still inhaling the warm morning breeze. He stopped the radio scan on a blues song that his uncle Jake used to play back in the day. He hummed along as the guitar player's harmony set the tone for the vocalist's apologetic chorus.

That gin and juice, it's got me loose, got me accused of something I didn't do,

That gin and juice, drinking all night long, had to meet this woman, but I should've been goin' home

His thick left bicep was posted on the truck door of the driver's side. He was marking his territory. This weekend, the island belonged to him.

*   *   *

2 Friday Morning

Kym entered through the rear of the beach house, after navigating across three miles of sand. Minutes earlier, she had stopped on the football-field length deck walkway long enough to catch her breath and wipe the perspiration from her brow. It had been years since she played softball at Cal-State Fullerton, and even longer since she had taken advantage of a sand workout at Laguna Beach, near her home in Mission Viejo. There were no spectacular cliff views to see here, but the water was warmer and calmer than the Pacific. It was the closest she would get to home for awhile, so she was adjusting to the fact that this would have to serve as a replacement for the trip to the Caribbean that she had foregone with her girlfriends to attend this company sojourn.

After waking up at eight-thirty in the morning, doing some Yoga exercises, and fast walking three miles in the humid Florida sun, Kym was ready for a relaxing shower. She removed the sweaty t-shirt and sports bra from her body, dropped her shorts and panties, and stepped into the shower that she purposely set on the cool side to control her sweating. She began brainstorming ideas in her head for the marketing project, hoping that her input would give the group a good jumpstart. She grabbed a travel bottle filled with white body wash and slowly worked the fresh smelling liquid over her legs and upper torso, until a rich lather appeared. When she reached her pubic hairs, she began to massage the creamy lather over her vagina in deliberate strokes, until the area was covered with small, white bubbles. Then, she began to cleanse the opening with her index and middle finger to rinse the smell of salt from her groin area. She moved back towards her clitoris, which had begun to swell, and slowly massaged it at an angle, until it began to redden with excitement. Kym closed her eyes, placed her left hand on the wall in front of her, and quickened her pace. Her heart rate began to increase, and small beads of sweat collected on her forehead. Her business thoughts were quickly transformed into thoughts of pure pleasure. An erotic landscape filled her subconscious. The muscles in her thighs began to tighten, and her toes started to curl. Suddenly, a rush of adrenaline filled her upper body, causing her chest to heave, and a trembling sensation ran through her body like an electric shock, causing her to lose grip of the shower wall and damn near slip face-first onto the shower floor. She took several deep breaths, rinsed again, and turned off the shower. As her euphoria began to subside, Kym dried off, brushed her teeth, freshened up, and slipped into a clean change of clothes. She opened the bathroom door, took another deep breath, and walked out into the foyer to head for the living area.

"Morning!" Felicia was walking by the hallway and caught Kym off guard.

"Oh!…Uh, good morning," Kym responded, as another quick adrenaline rush made her heart race and muscles jump.

"Sorry, didn't mean to scare you," Felicia said.

"That's okay. I was just getting out of the shower. I thought you guys were gone. I didn't see the truck in the driveway."

"Kelvin went to the store to get some things to put in the fridge. He's going to grill some hotdogs and hamburgers this afternoon after we meet. All business and no pleasure at this place would be a waste of scenery, don't you agree?"

"It sure would," Kym said, thinking to herself how pleasure had just paid her a visit.

She went to her room to put up her sweaty workout clothes, and laid on her back on the twin bed to recuperate for a minute. She gazed around at the room's Caribbean décor. The walls were painted in a soft, emerald green color, giving it a serene, tropical feel. The two beds were placed side-by-side, with matching comforters that matched the room's color with crème seashells added for decoration. On the wall, a framed picture of three men playing poker inside a dimly lit bistro on a deserted city corner cast a soft, midnight glow onto Kym's eyelids.

Just as the ceiling fan prepared to lull her into a late-morning siesta, Kym heard the quiet thumps of rhythm. As the thumps became a little louder, she suspected it was Kelvin. He had punished her and Felicia with his loud audio system Wednesday evening on the way to Albany, and again on the way to the beach yesterday. She almost wished she hadn't taken an extra day off and just driven her car instead. Felicia, however, had convinced her to ride with them to provide her company while Kelvin enjoyed a brief reunion with two of his partners who attended Albany State with him his freshman year.

Kym peeked out of the window and saw the metallic green monster truck pull into the carport, directly under her room and out of view. Two minutes later, a husky male voice followed the ring of the doorbell, eager to start the day's activities.

"Good morning, baby!" Kelvin's voice was filled with boyish excitement.

"Good morning back!" Felicia sounded more like a child than the everything woman that she was. The sound of a wet, sloppy lip collision signaled to Kym that it might be time to take that nap after all. Felicia's plans said otherwise.

"Kym!" Felicia said, in a firm, dry tone.

"I'll be there in a sec..." Kym responded, sounding unwilling and reluctant.

Kelvin walked back outside to retrieve the rest of the groceries, while Felicia prepared the dining table for business. At each seat, she placed a legal pad, black ink pen, and a calculator. Then, she walked to the nearby kitchen to prepare six glasses of water for her co-workers. Just like at Concepts, Felicia was Ms. Reliable. Always on time, the most dependable, and always willing to carry the load for her fellow associates. Those were quality traits of upper-management, Felicia believed, and as soon as she could finish her MBA program at Georgia State, that is exactly where she was going to go.

Kym shook the urge to sleep from her mind, and joined Felicia and Kelvin in the living area.

"Kym, could you help me make sandwiches for everyone? I don't think we should get started without something on our stomachs. They should be here any minute."

Kym reluctantly agreed, thinking that this was a perfect job for Kelvin, the one guest who could really count this weekend as a vacation. *He's a tag-along; he should automatically play housemaid,* Kym thought to herself. However, her hunger pains caused her rational thoughts to overpower her selfish thoughts, and she helped unpack the groceries.

*   *   *

After traveling through boon-hick, Florida, they reached a sign that read "St. George Island State Park, 9 Miles." The arrow pointed to the left, so Antoine took it. They soon began to traverse a bridge that reminded him of the MacArthur Causeway in Miami. He immediately began to feel homesick, reminiscing about his high school days at Carol City, the 183rd Street Flea Market, the Youth Fair, Conch Fritters, and his deceased grandparents. He was glad that his trip with Shauna to the Goombay Festival was only two weeks away.

"Ladies, rise and shine! We've got business to take care of."

Antoine's soft, assuring voice let them know that their fantasy with Mr. Sandman was up.

He turned the volume up a little on the car's stereo system, rolled the front windows down, and allowed the sounds of Kirk Franklin's song "Be Encouraged" to carry them over the bridge towards the island.

Leslie and Stacey slowly rose from their slumber, and joined the world of the living. Stacey reached into her purse to retrieve her mini-mirror and make-up kit. She was taught by her mother to never make an appearance in public looking worn-out. It was a trick that she had learned well. As she began applying her MAC products, Damien attempted to jump-start a conversation to mend his mess with Stacey.

"You ladies get some beauty rest?" He flashed a sincere smile as he peeked into the rearview mirror.

"Yeah," said Leslie, "but I could use some more."

Stacey was still upset with Damien, but wanted to remain cordial around Leslie and Antoine.

"Look at all the seagulls. There must be hundreds of 'em. This reminds me of back home."

Stacey's slight Louisiana drawl was apparent, as the French, Spanish, and African cultural influence over the centuries blended with English made some their A's sound like "Eh's," and their O's to come out sounding like thick "Oh's" and "Ah's," depending on what part of the word the letter fell on.

"What part of Louisiana are you from?" Leslie asked Stacey.

"Shreveport, Westside."

"How far is that from New Orleans?" Antoine asked.

"About six hours or so. It just depends on who's driving."

At the end of the bridge was a sign that read "Welcome to St. George Island: The Uncommon Florida." Antoine drove past the BP convenience store and made a right on West Gulfbeach Drive like Felicia had instructed. Various comments were made about the houses sitting on stilts, the sheriff's office that was located in a singlewide trailer, and the old white people whose stares made them feel unwelcome.

"You mean we have to spend the entire weekend here?" Stacey asked.

Leslie was just as disappointed. She was from Chicago's Southside, attended Hampton University, and worked back home at the Daily Defender before moving to Atlanta. The only time she really interacted with white people was at Concepts. And there, ethnicity was not a playing factor. "Marketing is a business," she was told by her advisor prior to graduation, "and the only characteristics absolutely necessary for career advancement is developing your skill set, and outwitting the competition." But this was not Atlanta. Here, the Confederate flag ruled. They were in the heart of Dixie. She could feel it. The uneasiness in the air told her so.

"Logan must have been pure crazy to send us down here. I don't care what this beach house looks like. They might try to use US for bait." Damien's joking comment sent scattered laughter throughout the car.

After traveling for almost two miles, they approached a sign that read Paradise Lane. They turned left, and drove past two quaint beach houses that looked weatherworn. At the end of the patchy road, sat a large, contemporary two-story beach house that was painted powder blue. It looked like it was a recent addition to the plethora of older-looking wooden beach houses that dotted this section of the island. Antoine parked under the stilts in the carport next to Felicia and Kelvin's truck, and they exited the vehicle.

"Damien, do you mind bringing our stuff up?" Stacey said, slamming the car door behind her. She wanted to embarrass him for the off-the-wall comment he made earlier in the morning, and her request put his chivalry on the spot.

"Yeah, sure," he reluctantly replied.

"The Tempest?" Antoine said, surprised at the name of their weekend home.

Stacey glanced at the sign nailed to the wall next to the door and giggled.

"It should say "Temporary." Because if the Ku Klux Klan rides by here tonight, that's how long my stay here is going to last."

"I know that's right," Leslie responded with a laugh, as she reached out to ring the doorbell. The single chime was immediately followed by a fast set of feet closing in on the front door. When the door swung open, a tall, thin frame greeted the weary travelers.

"Hey ladies!" Felicia sounded excited to see her co-workers.

"Hi, Felicia!" Leslie responded.

"Hi, Ms. Sampson," Stacey followed.

"Look Stacey, just because I'm a ticking time-bomb on the verge of menopause doesn't mean you have to call me by my last name. You guys come on in and make yourselves comfortable. We made you guys some sandwiches to eat before we get started. You know what they say, business before pleasure, and food before that."

"Umm Humm," Leslie nodded in agreement.

They entered the foyer area, and walked down the short hallway into a spacious living area.

"Are Damien and Antoine coming?" Felicia asked.

"Yeah, they're just grabbing our stuff to bring up. Antoine remembered to bring his laptop too," said Leslie.

"Great. Kym has hers as well. She just hooked it up over there on the table."

"Baby, you wanna help the guys with the bags? You know how ladies pack. They probably have three bags apiece." Felicia was joking, but she was right. Mommas always teach their daughters to be prepared for anything, just in case.

"Oh, I almost forgot to introduce my husband to you guys. Kelvin, meet two of my co-workers, Leslie and Stacey. They are working their way up the totem pole too, but if they stick near me, they'll soon be at the top, right ladies?"

"Pleasure to meet you," Kelvin said. He reached out with his right hand after wiping away the breadcrumbs, and greeted Leslie with a cordial handshake.

"I've heard all about you, Kelvin. You're the man that holds down the entire Hapeville plant. At least that's what Felicia tells us."

"Nah, just my assembly line. But it's nice to know my lady thinks so much of me," Kelvin responded with a generous smile.

He then directed his attention towards Stacey.

"Hi, Kelvin, nice to meet you." Stacey's outstretched hand almost went unnoticed. Kelvin's focus was on her beautiful, almond-shaped eyes and perfectly arched back, which seemed to elevate the fullness of her breasts. Her sleeveless white stretch shirt and khaki-colored stretch Capri pants looked perfect on her model-shaped five-foot seven-inch frame. Her perfume was alluring as well. It smelled similar to the one he noticed on a stripper two weeks ago when he and some co-workers went to Candies Gentlemen's Club to celebrate Mack's birthday.

"Pleasure's mine," Kelvin said, as he palmed Stacey's petite fingers with his thick hand. If it were 1885 she would have curtsied.

Felicia interrupted Kelvin's hot flash. "Kelvin, get your old behind out there and help those guys with the bags. Falling for that gentleman routine got me married with child," Felicia said, as she maneuvered her hands down her tall, slender frame like an airline stewardess to demonstrate that her body's slimness was now highlighted by a slight pouch on her stomach and sides. "If I hadn't fallen for that, I might have that two-seater Lexus by now, and be in the Bahamas enjoying tropical drinks with my girlfriends."

"Don't hate, don't hate," Kelvin responded, cutting his eyes at Felicia. His face displayed a mischievous grin. "Some women actually appreciate a hard working man when they see one."

Kelvin headed towards the door, and was greeted by Damien and Antoine, who were walking up the front steps dragging two large bags in each hand. Antoine had the extra burden of a laptop case strapped to his shoulder.

"Wassup fellas, let me grab a few of those bags off you," Kelvin said.

"We were wondering if you were going to help us, seeing as you're the low man on the totem pole this weekend," Antoine said. His snide comment didn't escape Kelvin's ears, but he played along anyway.

"I've heard a lot about you, Kelvin," Damien said as he relieved himself of two of the bags.

"I hope it's all been good. My wife can be hard on a brother sometimes." Kelvin grabbed one of Leslie's large bags from Antoine and started back towards the door.

"Name's Damien, nice to meet you." The burden of carrying the travel bags put the formality of handshakes on hold.

"Nice to meet you too. And you must be Antoine."

"Live and in the flesh," Antoine cockily responded. Kelvin closed the door behind them and helped everyone settle into their rooms before the meeting officially started.

*   *   *

3 Friday Afternoon

Kelvin sat Leslie's bag on her bed in one of the rear bedrooms downstairs. Damien and Antoine were downstairs too, debating about who would get the room with the fantastic view of the Gulf. Kelvin glanced at the clock that sat on the lamp stand. It read 12:17.

"Look, Antoine," Damien grumbled. "You know as well as I do that this room should be mine…it's not like you're gonna have anybody in here anyway, so you might as well give it up."

"You know what," Antoine shot back, "I'm not about to entertain myself with this petty foolishness. You can have the room. Just make sure you remember that the next time I need somebody to cover my workload. As a matter of fact, I'm taking a Friday off in two weeks to go to Miami, so I can use you then. That is, if you don't have a hangover and miss work again."

"Aiight, I see how you are. Your true colors are shining through. But I got you covered, B. Don't worry, I got you." Damien nodded and spoke quickly, as if to say *yeah right, hell if I will cover your load*. It was easy to tell when Damien got worked up. Anytime he started pacing quickly back and forth, and his Fortune 500 business vernacular vanished into his brain's ROM, trouble lay ahead. In its place entered the slick-talking hustler from Cleveland, the alter ego he longed to repress. But Darwin's Theory was rooted deep in his childhood experience. His two-bit con artist dad taught him everything he needed to know about surviving on the streets. He only went to college to satisfy the wishes of his mom and Ivy League stepfather, who used parental pressure and financial support to push him through Central State.

Kelvin exited Leslie's room just in time to catch the tail end of their room-jockeying session.

"Oooh-ooh, ya'll serious about that room, huh? Boy, I hope you two never break down in the middle of the desert and somebody needs to walk five miles for gas. The police would probably find two skeletons in the front seats, mouths wide open."

Antoine was not amused. "I didn't come here to argue, so let's go upstairs and handle this business so we can be done and enjoy this place."

"I agree," Kelvin said, and led their silent march up the stairwell to the living area.

As the three men appeared through the peach colored partition that marked a stairwell in the middle of the living area, Felicia decided to bring some order to all of the insignificant private activities that were occurring before her eyes. It was an all-too familiar scene at Concepts Marketing Group, and one of the main reasons Logan approached Felicia and Kym with the "team" idea for the Atlanta Convention and Visitor's Bureau project. They were reminded that teamwork is not only a well-established buzzword in today's corporate environment, but one of the most valued assets to ensure a company's success. This was not a foreign concept to Felicia. It was just absent at CMG. Then again, hiring folks as "Independent Associates," so the company could legally terminate their relationship with an employee without a detailed explanation or providing lucrative severance packages, was how CMG remained profitable and was recently listed by *American Demographics* magazine as one of the fastest rising marketing groups in the Southeast.

"All right people, let's get the show on the road. You've been fed, everybody has had some sleep, I presume, and I don't want to be working all day. This isn't exactly the place for that."

Felicia sounded more like a den mother, and at thirty-six, looked like one too. It didn't help that she needed a wardrobe change and a new hairstylist. But you couldn't tell her that a white ankle-length dress with floral prints wasn't cute; and although Kelvin loved Felicia with all his heart, he was tired of her bouffant hairstyle. As a matter of fact, he had been trying to convince her to try something different since 1993, the first year they met. He had even offered to subsidize her makeover.

Life's work, however, had been stealing away her free time as of late. Felicia had become a workaholic. She was the mother of an energetic boy, wife to an insatiable husband, den mother at work, a member of her church choir, president of a book club, and part-time student in an MBA program at Georgia State.

Wearing that many hats makes for a tired birthday girl; the bags under her eyes said that she was just plain worn out. But she couldn't stop now. She was too close to fulfilling her career goals. Truth be told, however, it felt as if her goals were moving further and further away. Call it penis envy. That's what Kelvin said. But Felicia was just trying to stay afloat, and keep up with the rest of buppy Atlanta. This was her personal definition of "Dirty South."

Eating two sandwiches piled high with deli meat, tomatoes, lettuce, and assorted condiments would make the average person very sleepy. At least that's the effect it had on Kelvin. He downed his food, along with a Coca-Cola C2 and a Snickers bar, and sat in an oak-colored wicker chair that faced rolling sand dunes dotted with nearby beach houses. The Gulf of Mexico sat slightly to his right. He gazed at the sweeping panoramic view offered by the living area's eight-foot sliding glass doors and picture windows. He leaned to his left, grabbed the television remote from off the cocktail table that sat in front of the tan chenille sofa, and turned on the TV. He tuned into ESPN's *SportsCenter* just in time for highlights of the NBA basketball playoffs. As he slumped back into the chair's inviting cushion, the voices coming from the television became garbled. With the remote control placed securely above his waist, Kelvin nodded a few times before joining the sleep fairy for an afternoon siesta.

Damien was in the kitchen holding a casual conversation with Leslie, and Antoine was in the sitting room next to the foyer checking in with Shauna to inform her of their safe arrival.

Stacey was at the dining table finishing her lunch and browsing through her *Black Hair* magazine. Kym was at the other end of the table checking her e-mail on the laptop. She pecked out a quick response to a friend regarding a dinner date for next week.

Can do; Look, I've got to go. Meeting about to begin... Keep the cat clean for me, okay?
WBS. By the way, tab's on U (LOL ☺).

MzKym

She closed out of her e-mail service, and waited for everyone to join her and Stacey at the table. She wondered if her cat Spice, a Blue Smoke Persian, was tearing up her living room.

I hope they're showing something good on Animal Planet, she thought to herself, remembering that she had turned her television on before she left. Spice was pretty well trained, but was known to be a misfit in her absence.

As soon as everyone made it to the table, Felicia made it clear that she was not going to tolerate filibustering, as she knew the weekend would be wasted if everyone got too comfortable.

"Look, I'm not trying to be abrasive towards anyone here, but we need to be prompt this weekend. This is the first time I've been without my child for five months, and I would really like to enjoy this place. If we set a limit to this meeting, say two hours, and meet again tomorrow, we can have this proposal finished and on Logan's desk by Monday morning, okay?"

Everyone nodded and mumbled in agreement, and the meeting commenced.

"So what exactly is it that we're proposing?" asked Damien, sounding concerned.

"We have won a bid for a major project with the Atlanta Convention and Visitor's Bureau to overhaul its marketing plan," Felicia explained.

"As you know, the city has been in the red for more than two years and desperately needs vehicles for increased revenue. They are overhauling the city's water infrastructure at an estimated cost of almost four billion dollars…"

Kym chimed in. "And they've been searching for ways to cut direct costs to residents so they won't move out of Fulton into the other metro counties."

"But what about the feds; isn't Uncle Sam supposed to help out?" Antoine asked.

"Yes," Felicia answered, "but they've only promised a billion. The other money is coming from loans, taxes, and ratepayers. But the federal money can be pulled at any time, because of the military investment overseas and abroad. Ever since September 11th, we have been trying to police the world, and that has depleted the nation's budget. As a matter of fact, over half of this year's budget will go directly to the military."

"Damn, Felicia, sounds like you've done your research," Damien playfully chided. "I have," Felicia replied, "and you'd better too. One of my professors at Georgia State discusses the financial impact of terrorism and the U.S. Homeland Security policy every time we meet. He makes it a requirement for us to watch MSNBC, CNN, or Fox News Channel for thirty minutes per day so he can facilitate classroom discussions. He's worried that Social Security will be dried up in less than ten years, which will leave him with only a pension fund and individual investments to retire with."

Stacey listened quietly to the exchange of information being forwarded across the table between her co-workers, and directed a question to Felicia.

"So basically, when I retire, if I haven't saved or invested my money right, then I'm screwed?"

"Yes, for a lack of better words, you are," Felicia replied.

Damien thought about the last two words out of Stacey's sexy Lipglass coated lips, and wished he could do that to her.

Antoine continued the conversation. "So what does all of this financial doom and gloom have to do with this project?"

"Glad you asked," Felicia said. "It's well known in Atlanta as well as other major cities, that their tourism bureaus do not fully cater to the needs of African-Americans, and other minorities. All you have to do is check the website and you will see that we have been excluded from their invitation."

"What's the website?" Antoine asked, as he prepared to type the address into his web browser.

"It's www.acvb.net." Antoine typed in the address and pushed the enter button on his laptop.

"I see black people on here," Antoine said.

"True, but look a little further into the site, and you will see what the concern is about. You see the section for multicultural visitors?" Felicia asked.

"No," Antoine replied. "It's there," Felicia continued, "but you have to dig deep into the site. "You have to go to the visitor's section, and then find the multicultural information link. Once you do that, you have to click another link that takes you to a separate website that deals with Atlanta's black heritage"

"Damn, you 'gotta go real deep into that bad boy to find the black stuff," Damien remarked. He and Leslie had gotten up and were standing over Antoine's shoulder peering into the computer screen.

"You see," Leslie said, "there's the hidden racism. Atlanta is sixty percent black, but our section of the website is way in the back, like that driver wanted Rosa Parks on that bus."

"And they know good and well that the average visitor won't surf that deep into a site unless the link is right there on the front page," Damien added.

"But wait, there's more," Felicia said. She was on a roll now, feeling comfortable in her position as team lead.

"Look at the list of suppliers. How many African-American businesses can you find? How many black caterers?"

"None, that I can tell," Antoine said, sounding surprised.

"Exactly. That's why we have to incorporate within our plan opportunities for more minority vendors with the city. The NAACP and local politicians have been putting pressure on city hall to increase minority participation in city services. If we devise a plan for the bureau that will welcome black businesses, conventions, and leisure travelers with open arms, we could force a coup from other cities and increase the amount of revenue in the city's coffers at the same time."

This conversation was right down Leslie's ally. But she was taught at an early age to be cautious when it came to dealing with white folks, especially on the job.

"Okay, forgive me for being naïve Felicia, but since when did Concepts start trying to come up with ways to make Atlanta more diverse? Last time I checked there were only twelve blacks on our staff of over a hundred, including a secretary and a maintenance man. That means they are just meeting their quota for Affirmative-Action."

Kym cut in before Felicia could answer. "Since the CVB decided to outsource their work. They didn't want to use their staff. They wanted to bring someone in from the outside to prove that they are truly committed to this plan. Plus, this would look real nice in the Concepts portfolio. It's a PR job."

"I see," Leslie said. "So Atlanta gets financially strapped, and they want to ride our backs to get them out of their predicament." Leslie spoke in a slow, deliberate tone. "That's probably how some of us got our jobs, right Kym?"

"What do you mean?" Kym asked. Her eyes narrowed, and her face frowned with concern.

"You know what I mean," Leslie continued. "For centuries, we," Leslie said, while pointing her finger around to everyone except Kym, "have been toiling in the cotton fields, fighting segregation, dying for equal rights, protesting for Affirmative-Action, and trying to build ourselves up economically, just to have America pass us the crumbs so it can unravel ITS portfolio to the world and say, "Look at us! Look at what we've done for our minorities!" While all the while, it's really a PR job, just like you said, and at the end of the day we still have nothing to show for it."

Kym's face began to redden, her multicultural background highlighted for all to see. She sensed Leslie's direction, and felt alone again, just as she had back in California. She always tried to fit in, but never quite could.

"Look at you." Leslie stared Kym up and down, and began to assault her in a verbal tirade reminiscent of Louis Farrakhan at the Million Man March. "I'm willing to bet that when you were in college, you had it made. You probably had all kinds of scholarships, didn't you?"

A bewildered Kym stared at Leslie but kept her composure.

"As a matter of fact Leslie, I was on scholarship for softball and academics."

"Good for you," Leslie replied, clapping as she spoke. "Let me ask you then; when you checked the race box on your application, did you check African-American, Asian, or other?"

If someone had dropped a hairpin it would have caused an earthquake in the house. Besides the low hum of the television, the room was silent. Kelvin's nap-taking session had turned into a closed-eyes surveillance operation; he was all ears.

Felicia wanted badly to end Leslie's interrogation of Kym. Besides, she and Kym held seniority over their neophyte co-workers. Her inner-ambitions to obtain a mid-level management position at Concepts, however, called for some sacrifice. Unfortunately, Kym was the lamb.

Kym stared in disbelief at Leslie, and then at the eight other hungry eyes that visually mutilated her. She replied with an answer that was politically correct, but would immediately destroy her standing as "one of them."

"What I checked is my business."

Stacey looked down at the table, and shook her head in disbelief. Antoine stared at Kym and muttered "Umph." Damien's left eyebrow rose with concern, as he leaned back in his chair and folded his arms across his chest. Felicia stared at the table too, as she silently contemplated what had just happened.

It had never been easy for Kym to "belong" to either one of her ethnic groups. Blacks always wanted her to "fit in" by assimilating into their social fabric, and Koreans treated her as if she was infected with a deadly virus. The only group outside of her home that ever accepted Kym as a person, were whites. She had always felt alienated for being different, and her exterior beauty hid the immense pain that she felt inside. It was times like this that made her want to curl up and die. That way, she wouldn't have to answer any more questions.

Leslie, who by now was more fired up than a Mississippi tent revival, continued her verbal barrage.

"Another Tiger Woods. Trying to be something you're not. Try walking through Birmingham, Alabama at midnight, and tell the police you're not black. You've got some nerve. I'll bet that's why Logan sent you down here this weekend, for PR. Because the moment the Supreme Court overturns Affirmative Action, we'll all be swimming backwards down the creek, except for you. You fit in; because you talk like them, walk like them, and think like them. At the end of the day, you are like them, because you could care less about the black community and its concerns, isn't that right?"

Felicia knew it was time to play peacemaker and restore order. She decided to cut short Leslie's tirade and try to mend any ill feelings that circulated among the room's occupants.

"Look, that's enough; nobody in here knows what Kym has had to go through to reach this point in her career. It's hard enough just being a woman in corporate America. We have to work twice as hard, learn twice as much, and be three times as willing to do the things men don't like to do. Shoot, they might as well call me a high priced secretary with all of the paperwork that comes across my desk, only for a man to benefit from my hard work."

"Amen, sistah!" Antoine yelled out, standing and twirl hopping with one hand in the air, imitating the shout section of his church. His action brought laughter to the room, a much-needed reprieve to the thick tension that held their meeting hostage.

Leslie was still visibly upset, and heaved a full breath of air to calm her nerves. Kym expressed a wry smile. She knew that the rest of her weekend here would have to be played out carefully. She was no longer trusted.

*   *   *

Kelvin was awake now. He looked at the time above the TV on a round, brown wall clock. It read 1:15. He needed to use it, so he put down the remote and headed for the master bedroom, trying to avoid eye contact with the table's occupants, especially Kym.

"Okay," Felicia said, "now that we know each other informally, let's be professional and work towards accomplishing our goal."

"So is that it?" Damien asked, questioning the purpose of the project. "We just need to overhaul their website to cater to African-Americans?"

"No," Felicia responded, "actually, it isn't. That's just one part of it, the small part really. As you all know, this is still a business, and if the money isn't there, it doesn't matter if the target demographic is blue, black, brown, white, purple, or yellow. An area sample was conducted last year to determine which cities within a five hundred mile radius of Atlanta had the largest amount of repeat visitors and tourists. Part of our job is to devise a way to keep the repeat visitors and tourists, and attract new ones as well. With the new aquarium and World of Coke, that won't be difficult, but the marketing will be crucial, especially when the city budget is tight."

"We've got the Falcons too," said Stacey. "I know people who would kill for season tickets, and Michael Vick? Chiiild Puhlease. That's the prettiest black face a man could have. And he's fiiiine—" Stacey fanned her face with a napkin as the pitch of her voice escalated to emphasize the word fine.

"Yeah, yeah, yadda-yadda. Maybe he can stay healthy THIS season," Damien said sarcastically. He simulated a yawn, as if he was offended because she acted like the men in her presence were invisible.

Felicia, however, was impressed. Finally, some forward progress was being made.

"No, No," Felicia said, validating Stacey's adoration of the Falcon's star player.

"She's got a point. We SHOULD use the Falcons as a marketing tool for the city, incorporate it into our proposal, maybe even as the centerpiece, being that they're so popular now."

"Yeah, like how Dallas was "America's Team" back in the day, until they found out half of 'em were either pushing, or using dope."

Everyone's head turned towards the hallway to where Kelvin's voice was. He was returning from his bathroom break.

"Sorry to interrupt 'cha, but I couldn't help but overhear your conversation."

"That's okay Kelvin," Kym responded, trying to deflect the oddball status to someone other than herself. "Elaborate on that, please."

"I'm just saying, you can make the Falcons the new America's Team. All of the players are pretty much squeaky-clean, they've got a group of bona-fide stars, and they're going deep into the playoffs this year, hopefully even the Super Bowl. Plus, the Julios on Buford Highway support 'em. Make them popular in Mexico, and you've got 'em."

"So you're a marketing major now, huh?" Antoine asked Kelvin, trying to be sarcastic.

"No, I just know what I see," Kelvin answered matter-of-factly. He stood behind Felicia at the head of the table, his thick, two hundred fifteen-pound frame casting a large shadow on the wall behind them.

"I tailgate with my co-workers at every game. The ones who can't get in just hang out in the parking deck and watch the game on their portable TV's. Used to be a time you couldn't pay somebody to see a Falcons game. Kinda like the Hawks."

Damien was impressed. "Umm. And isn't the Super Bowl in Tennessee this year?"

"Yep. So if the Falcons win home field advantage, guess what?"

"What?" A three-person chorus answered.

"The NFC Championship will be played right here in ATL baby," Kelvin said. His hands became demonstrative. His arms were spread out like a bird, with each index finger extended; he wagged his hands frantically up and down to accentuate his point. He became so excited, he forgot he was in Florida.

"So?" Antoine said, trying to throw haterade in Kelvin's game.

"So you can include a gigantic party weekend in your plan, like a just-in-case scenario, sponsored by the City of Atlanta and the Visitor's bureau, that'll take advantage of the opportunity and make tons of money. You know how many ballers would come through the ATL on the way to the Super Bowl?" Kelvin said.

Kelvin had everyone's attention now. His Leo personality was now on full display, his impetuous temperament almost making him forget that he wasn't with them.

"It would be bigger than the All-Star game a few years ago." Kelvin was referring to the NBA All-Star weekend in 2003 that virtually shut the entire city down.

"But I ain't responsible for no traffic jams." Kelvin let out a big smile, and walked away from the table, heading towards the kitchen.

"That's an excellent idea, baby." Felicia said. She was impressed. *That's worthy of a "coochie coupon,"* she thought to herself. She hadn't broken Kelvin off with sex in almost two weeks, because she was so busy doing the things that she needed to do, like preparing for finals at State, packing Jordan's clothes for his weekend stay at her girlfriend Apreal's, finishing the latest E. Lynn Harris novel for the book club meeting next week, grocery shopping, attending choir rehearsal, and reviewing specifications of the marketing project with Logan and Kym.

"I tell you what guys; I think this is a good time for us to jot our ideas down on the notepads that I gave you. We'll take about thirty minutes, and then Kym and I will collect your input. Tomorrow, we can meet once more to discuss the details, and then Kym and I will type the proposal up. How's that sound?" Felicia said.

Everyone nodded in agreement.

"Stacey, you're in advertising, right?" Felicia asked.

"Yes."

"Can you work on that part with Kym? The rest of us will focus on the marketing, demographics, cost, and the website layout."

"Cool."

Teamwork suddenly became everyone's friend. It was common for consultants at Concepts to jockey their way past others for lucrative accounts. A lot of backstabbing occurs in that type of environment. Small teams had formed, alliances that would rival the reality show *Survivor*, all in the name of personal success. But this new team was strong. Their silence illuminated their resolve. They were determined to show their superiors and other associates at Concepts that they were more than qualified for their positions. And this would be the project to prove it.

While they worked on the marketing plan, Kelvin prepared to season the hamburger meat for the grill. The oak wood cabinets, gray and black L-shaped granite counter top, and black refrigerator were all unexpected luxuries for Kelvin. He didn't know exactly what to expect, but this was good. He loved to cook, and was the main grill master when he and his co-workers from Ford tailgated during football season. Kelvin opened each cabinet door to check its contents, and forage for seasonings. He decided on paprika, garlic salt, thyme, and a little pepper. He pulled a bowl and a large glass dish from one of the bottom cabinets, washed his hands, and went to work.

Still in disbelief about the beauty of the island, Kelvin alternated the focus of his eyes between the raw hamburger meat and the beach. Puffy clouds painted against the bright, electric blue sky seemed to highlight the activity occurring below. Pelicans floating in place high above the water made sudden screams towards unsuspecting marine life, shooting like pencil-bombs with their wings folded in. The crash of their bodies against God's gigantic pool threw the water into disarray. It was difficult to tell whether their missions were successful or not. The deck walkway stood proud, but weatherworn. Tall blades of saw grass lapped at the sides of the walkway, like paid sentries waiting to interrogate human sand seekers.

This is fantastic, Kelvin thought to himself, wondering what else he had missed while growing up in a dysfunctional urban environment. He swept his head 180 degrees to his left, marveling at the layout of the living area. The peach staircase sat in the middle; beyond that was the chair he had been sitting in, a tan colored sofa and loveseat, and the hallway that led to the master bedroom. Near the wall, between the wicker chair and the stairwell sat a black dining table full of busy corporate bees. He admired the open floor plan, and made a mental note to himself that he would come back with his family one day soon. Real soon.

"Anybody thirsty?" Kelvin said, wanting to feel like he was playing a part in the weekend operation.

"I'll take another glass of water," Felicia replied.

"Me too," said Kym.

"Right here bruh," Damien said, as he lifted his left hand in the air like he was still in grade school. His endearing salutation was a result of him pledging Kappa in college. He said it out of habit now. Plus, Kelvin was pretty cool, Damien thought. Maybe he could be an honorary bruh.

Kelvin finished seasoning the meat, washed his hands again, and walked over to the table to pour water from the gallon-sized plastic jug into the glasses of the thirsty thinkers.

Stacey gave Kelvin a friendly smile, and he returned to his hermit hole in the kitchen, trying to keep busy.

Felicia glanced at her brown pleather Wal-Mart wristwatch. It read 2:05.

"Okay you guys; let's wrap this thing up. I'm not trying to work all day. Plus, my stomach will be growling soon, and I need to feed myself before I see anything on this island!"

"Alright sistuh girl!" Leslie replied, and gave Felicia a high hand slap across the table.

After a few minutes, everyone had given their notepads to Felicia and Kym to glance over and put away until tomorrow. Antoine powered off his laptop, pulled out his memory stick, and clicked it onto his key chain. Kym soon followed, after she saved the meeting notes on her word processing program and typed a few words to her friend on her instant messenger.

Brrrlingg! The sound of a rolling bell was made after each entry was posted to alert the recipient to pay attention.

NvrtlU2b: so r u finished?
MzKym: Just got...
NvrtlU2b: how'd it go?
MzKym: It went.
NvrtlU2b: how about cheesecake factory when you get back?
MzKym: Cool, it's on u. ☺ LOL
NvrtlU2b: okay, fine. monday night?
MzKym: That's fine. Look, gotta go. HAK
NvrtlU2b: hugs and kisses back. bye!

Kym powered off, and closed her laptop. She excused herself to the bedroom she was sharing with Stacey. She was exhausted. She stayed up late last night e-mailing, chatting, and browsing the Internet. She rarely slept for more than five hours, a routine she copied from her father, a military retiree. The Army taught him all about discipline, work ethic, and living by strict routines. He passed that along to Kym through osmosis. But she was older now. At thirty-four, she was no longer a spring chicken.

It seemed like yesterday she was catching the fly balls of her opponents in right field. Her team finished near the top of their collegiate softball conference. But now, she was near the apex of her physical life, and she could tell. She felt things in her body that weren't there fifteen years ago. She wondered if it would ever be possible to settle down and have a baby. The chase for financial and professional success might have ruined that. As she slowly drifted off to sleep, a million thoughts crossed and weaved through her mind.

One thing's for sure, she thought, as her eyelids began to weigh down. *If I never have children, the world will be a better place. At least no one will be able to question their racial allegiance because of how they look.* A solitary teardrop formed in Kym's right eye and rolled down her cheek. It came to a rest, leaving a tiny, salty stain on her white pillow. She balled up into the fetal position, pulled the covers around her shoulders, and fell asleep.

* * *

4 Friday Afternoon

The mid-afternoon sun cast its vibrant spring energy onto the island. The temperature was near its predicted high of 85, and a steady breeze whipped the shoreline, as the sun began its long descent towards the Gulf's quiet waves. Kelvin walked outside onto the large deck that surrounded the back half of the beach house. A black charcoal grill sat to his right around the corner, waiting to be used. He enjoyed the warm breeze that laughed across his face, and the occasional wind gust that whipped his t-shirt into a frenzy. He walked around the corner, removed the bag of charcoals and hickory-flavored wood chips from the brown paper grocery bag he was holding, and began preparations for his "Kelvin Burgers," as he called them. He didn't have a name for his hotdogs yet, but when he grilled them, they had to be crispy and black around the exterior.

Stacey took a change of clothes and a towel into the foyer bathroom, and took a shower. Damien, and then Antoine did the same in the downstairs bathroom that was situated across from the wall of Leslie's room in a small hallway. Leslie settled in a white lounge chair on the downstairs deck to gather her thoughts and read the *Atlanta Daily World*, an African-American newspaper that kept her in tune with the happenings of her people. She folded the pages in half so the newspaper wouldn't blow away, and focused her energy on an article about another teenage basketball phenom who was projected to go number one in the NBA draft next month. As she read through his personal career stats, physical attributes, and a story about his team's run to a state championship, she wondered what kind of role model he would make as another teenaged, black multi-millionaire. Her thoughts returned to the summers she spent back home in Chicago volunteering at Westside Prep, the school founded by Marva Collins, and several public schools on the Southside.

There was a stark contrast, she thought to herself, in how the kids at Westside learned compared to the kids at the public schools. Students at Westside studied Shakespeare before entering middle school. Teachers could not sit idly at their desks, because they didn't have any. The Westside model emphasized high teaching standards, personal responsibility, and student achievement. Kids at the public schools, however, threw paper and assaulted each other in the hallways, openly disrespected their teachers, gossiped during class, and rarely brought pencils to write with, paper to write on, or textbooks to study from.

As a classroom volunteer during the last two years of the Chicago Bulls title runs, she clearly remembered a question being asked by a teacher to her sixth-grade male pupils the first day of class in one particular public school.

"How many of you want to be doctors?" she asked enthusiastically. One raised his hand.

"How many want to be lawyers?" Two raised their hands.

"How many plan on going to college and graduating?" Eight was the count. Finally, she asked the question she set them up for, the one she knew would elicit the most responses.

"How many of you plan on going to the NBA and being the next Michael Jordan?"

"Ooh! Ooh!" The chorus of male voices sang, as hands shot up like rockets, and legs frantically rocked, lifting chairs from their foundations. A mad scramble ensued to see who could get the teacher's attention first. Leslie conducted an unofficial hand count. Sixteen, one shy of being unanimous.

Leslie was dismayed. It was this same disillusionment that resulted in her brother Irwin's death in a gun battle with gang bangers at a convenience store off 79th. She was only twelve at the time, but her soul was shattered. She expected more from her older brother, whose nickname was "Justice." Only when she had gotten older, did she realize that his nickname was no longer connected to her parent's involvement in the Black Panther movement during the early seventies.

One of her brother's friends told her shortly after her high school graduation that Irwin had gotten involved with the Vice Lords gang in middle school, and was banging by the time he reached ninth grade. "Justice," she was told, was the same moniker with a new definition. It stood for the fury in which he punished his rivals when they were caught slipping.

Shortly after Leslie enrolled at Hampton University, she decided to honor her parent's heritage by getting a tattoo placed on her right ankle. It was a Black Panther. She promised herself that she would never forget where she came from, no matter how successful she became. It was a promise that became her personal paradox. It's the reason why she jumped off into Kym for being different. It was the reason she felt uncomfortable working in corporate America. It was also the reason why she couldn't find a good man. The good men, she blindly assumed, the ones who didn't forget their heritage, were either broke, expected their wives to be submissive, or were locked up in Uncle Sam's penal system. Feeling depressed, she put her newspaper down, stared out into the Gulf, and swallowed her pain.

Felicia joined Kelvin on the upstairs deck, and pretended to have some grill skills.

"Let me get the fire started baby," she remarked, as she playfully bumped into Kelvin with her left hip.

"Girl, you're gonna blow this whole house up if I give you this fire." Kelvin was laughing as he held the long, red cylinder container full of fireplace matches away from Felicia with his left hand, and pushed her away with his right.

He could tell when Felicia was horny. She always flirted when she wanted some. Not like a man, who could fuck at the drop of a dime.

"Watch out," Kelvin said, as he struck a match on the bottom of the container and touched it to several spots around the wood chip-covered charcoal pyramid. He was glad that he purchased self-lighting charcoal. The last time he barbecued, he squirted a little too much lighter fluid on the charcoal, and almost blew his face up.

Kelvin waited for the fire to settle and transform the corners of the charcoals into glowing embers. When he saw some white ashes, Kelvin knew it was time to burn. He replaced the grill cover, opened the vent, and stepped back to the deck's rail. As soon as he saw a white plume of smoke, he smiled with satisfaction. *It's on,* he thought to himself.

"I'm going back inside," Felicia said. "It's hot out here. Let me know if you need anything, okay? By the way, I really appreciate the input during the meeting. You might not work with us, but your opinion was greatly appreciated. I love you." Felicia gave Kelvin a loving smack on the cheek, opened one of the sliding glass doors, and disappeared inside the beach house to relax and enjoy some A.C.

Ten minutes later, Kelvin was playing host to a personal barbeque fest. His audience consisted of five hotdogs, and three hamburgers. The juice from the hamburger meat poured over the hot ashes, making a sound similar to hot water running over a pot of boiling rice. A "cafeteria lady" look was painted on his face with a glare that said *don't mess with this operation.*

Just then, Stacey opened the glass sliding door, and walked out onto the deck resembling a runway model in Milan. Her long, straight mane sat perfectly on her medium-sized head. A shiny lotion that seemed to wrap her body's portrait into a beautiful brown package highlighted her mocha-colored skin. Her shoulders were perfectly aligned, and her toes were painted with a French pedicure. She had the perfect accessories to qualify her as a dime-piece. When her soft, Louisiana voice spoke, it took Kelvin to heaven.

"Hey Kelvin," she said, as she sat in a long, white lounge chair near the corner where Kelvin stood.

"S'up Stacey," Kelvin said, trying to keep his cool.

Stacey opened her *Black Hair* magazine and perused its contents. She wanted to be prepared if any agents from her recent open calls wanted her to work next week. She was sure business was about to pick up, because her web design hobby had fueled her desire to develop her own website. Just last month, she paid for her site to join the gazillions of others in cyberspace, in hopes that she could leave her corporate job forever.

Kelvin was definitely intrigued by this mystery girl, and even though he was married, he felt the urge to flirt from time to time. As a matter of fact, his Uncle Jake told him back in the day that God didn't plan for man to have just one woman. If that were the case, he told him, he would have stopped with Eve. Uncle Jake was crazy. At least that's what his momma used to say.

"What's that you're reading?" Kelvin asked, as he slowly approached Stacey's chill out spot. "*Black Hair* magazine," Stacey responded, as she looked up and met Kelvin's innocent, lustful gaze.

Kelvin peeked at the open pages of the magazine and feigned interest in its contents.

"Look at those styles. I could never be a hair stylist. I'd have somebody suing me for false advertising. I'll have your hair parted on one side, braided on the other. Probably put two ponytails in the back, too."

Stacey cracked up. "What would you call your business?"

"I'd call it "Dammit I Can't Do Hair," Kelvin said. His look was both funny and serious at the same time. Stacey laughed so hard she almost turned her lounge chair over.

"How do they get their hair to look like that?" Kelvin asked, pointing towards the open magazine.

"You mean, the technical process of it?"

"Yeah."

"Well, first you have to decide on a hair style. If you want something short, you may be able to get it done without weave. If you want something long or funky, you probably have to get some weave, unless you're mixed with Indian."

"Oh, really," Kelvin said.

"Yeah." Stacey was ready to sign Kelvin up for Hair 101. It was obvious from looking at Felicia's tired hairstyle that this man needed a lesson.

"You see this?" Stacey said, as she pointed to a picture of an actress with long, flowing, shoulder-length hair.

"Yeah."

"This is a layered cut with braided weave. There's no way her hair is that long naturally."

"I see. Show me another one," Kelvin said.

Stacey flipped a few pages, stopping at a picture of a model wearing a wavy cap weave.

"You see this girl?" Stacey asked.

"Yeah."

"This is a cap weave. Basically the hair is attached to a cap, and you just put it on your head, fluff it and go."

"So you don't even have to waste all that time in front of a mirror in the mornings if you don't have to?"

"Nope. But that's your preference."

Kelvin reached into his memory bank and thought about all the mornings that Felicia complained about not having enough time to get ready for work. Maybe if he brought her a cap weave, he thought, she wouldn't have to rush out of the door every morning instead of breaking him off. He was all ears.

"And this one," Stacey said, as she flipped to another page. "This is what I want next week if Hennessy or one of my other prospects calls me back."

"Hennessy?" Kelvin asked, with a surprised look on his face.

"Yeah, I model on the side. I just finished my own website too."

"Oh, really. I ain't mad you, girl. If I looked like you, I'd be marching through downtown Paris talkin' 'bout "Here I am! I'm the one you've been looking for! Damn Tyra! Don't nobody want that alien-head girl! I'd be struttin' my stuff like a champion thoroughbred. Pleeze b'leeve it." Kelvin had his hands around his mouth like a bugle, yelling at the birds that sang playfully while encircling each other twenty yards out from the deck.

Stacey got a good laugh from Kelvin's antics, and stood up to get a view of the ocean.

"That sure is pretty," Stacey said, as she gazed across the majestic scenery.

"Yes it is," Kelvin replied, as he honed his sights once again on the beautiful swan that stood next to him. *Damn, she's fine,* Kelvin thought to himself. *If I wasn't married I'd...*

She was wearing a thin, white sundress and orange thong panties. Her thong slides with three-inch heels allowed her perfectly curved behind and calves to pose in their beautiful, sexy splendor. A gust of wind suddenly blew towards Stacey, in an attempt to expose her exquisite bronze underside. She stood ready, eager to accept nature's fresh breath.

Kelvin stared, wide-eyed and bewildered. Stacey's long black silky hair blew wildly around her face. Her dress lapped to and fro, up and down, exposing her hips for Kelvin to savor. She lifted her right hand, and motioned for Kelvin to approach, licking the fullness of her lips with her soft tongue. Hesitant, Kelvin stepped forward towards his walk with destiny. As she eagerly awaited his approach, the entire beach house was sucked away into eternity like a scene out of *The Matrix*. It was immediately replaced by the warm, inviting waters of an isolated tropical island. They were finally alone, ready to enjoy each other's essence in the tranquility of paradise. Just as Kelvin took another step, a loud voice screamed in a high shrill. It was powerful enough to shatter his erotic daydream.

"Kelvin!!"

It was Felicia. Kelvin's muscles twitched in his large frame, causing him to jump. He turned just in time to see what was making Felicia panic. The fire on the grill had re-ignited after receiving a healthy dose of oxygen from the gusts of wind that flew from the beach, and some fat drippings from the hamburger meat. Kelvin had opened the vent too far, and a dancing fire was visible through the gang of grayish smoke that plumed upwards in all directions.

Kelvin rushed over, grabbed a water bottle from the cooler that sat near the grill, quickly unscrewed the top, and poured its contents through the grill vent. He lifted the top back, and poured the rest over the remains of the dry, ashy Kelvin Burgers and used-to-be hotdogs. Embarrassment immediately became Kelvin's middle name. He tried his best to cover up his culinary negligence, knowing that his stupidity was to blame.

"Damn, I didn't even realize it was cooking that fast," he said.

Felicia pulled him inside by his arm, pursed her lips, and whispered angrily inside his ear.

"If you weren't paying so much attention to that damn girl, maybe you could get something done," she said.

Felicia rarely cursed. That's how Kelvin could tell if she was genuinely upset. What he didn't know, however, is that she had created a mental note to herself. She was going to add a gym membership to her to-do list starting next week. She couldn't believe that having Jordan had caused her body to deteriorate. All Felicia wanted was for Kelvin to lust for her in the same way.

*   *   *

Damien needed a beer. After listening to gospel music from Thomasville to St. George Island, his nerves were shaken. Not that he didn't respect the Lord's work, but it was Friday. He was used to listening to the Ryan Cameron Morning show on 107.9 or Frank Ski and the crew on V-103. They were known to have a good laugh, and play some jammin' music, too. He walked upstairs and greeted Felicia and Kelvin, just as she was turning Kelvin's bicep loose.

"I didn't interrupt anything, did I?" Damien said.

"Naw, man. Felicia was just telling me how much she adored my cooking, that's all."

Kelvin was a master of verbal manipulation. He knew how to squeeze himself out of a jam. It was a skill he utilized often in high school, when he realized that his academic aptitude was not up to par, compared to most of his friends. His charm often matched his wit, resulting in a gregarious personality that allowed him to talk himself into or out of just about any situation.

"Smells like you're cooking something alright," Damien said, simultaneously sniffing the overdone air. He was definitely trying to be funny.

"Look, you want something from the store?" Damien asked. "I'm going to get some beer. No sense in being down here without a cold one. It'll go good with that pool table downstairs."

"Oooh, you play?" Kelvin asked, in a childlike tone.

"Hell yeah I play. When I get back, we'll run a few. How 'bout that?"

Kelvin was excited about the prospect of getting down on the billiards table. He'd been so busy lately trying to keep the household up while Felicia attended classes that he didn't have time to hang out with the boys as much as he used to.

"Tell you what. You go and get those cold ones, and I'll tighten you up on this grill. By the time you get back, you'll be honored to have a taste of my world famous "Kelvin Burgers.""

"We'll see." Damien grabbed the keys to the company car from off the table, and skirted towards the door into the afternoon haze.

Felicia was just about to jump back into Kelvin's personal space when a female silhouette emerged from the stairwell.

"Alright Kelvin, I smell the food, is it ready?" Leslie asked.

"I had a slight accident. I'll have you tightened up in a minute though," Kelvin said.

With her arms folded, Felicia gave Kelvin an x-ray stare, rolled her eyes back, and with the snap of her head, jump-started herself into the master bedroom.

"What's wrong with her?" Leslie said, trying to delicately referee a possible domestic dispute.

"Nothing," Kelvin said. "She's just mad that I can cook better than her, that's all."

Leslie's right eyebrow rose enough to produce crinkles in her forehead. Her puzzled look was enough for Kelvin to know that his explanation was a crock of shit.

Damien cranked up the MACH sound system on the Ford Taurus, and absorbed the sights of St. George. It was the weekend prior to the Memorial Day holiday, and he could tell. Most of the beach houses were at full capacity. He squinted his eyes long enough to peep license tags from across the United States, but mostly from up North. Ohio, Illinois, Michigan, Virginia. He also observed a few from down South. Florida, Georgia, Alabama, North Carolina.

His "Best of Lil John" CD was cranking out of the speakers full tilt. He brought the bootleg CD from a young hustler outside of the Underground Mall a few months ago for five dollars, so he didn't care if it got scratched up from playing it too much. It's always funny watching a Northerner get crunk to Southern rap music, because the music is so different. People look at Southern rap videos and think that it's easy to bounce in sync with the grungy 808 beats. That's what the teenage "wiggers" must have thought when they saw Damien pass by B.J.'s Pizza. A song called "B.I." was playing through the system's speakers, but his head nodding was a little off. It seemed like he was bouncing to his own rhythm, but the expression on his face said he didn't care. And the wild look in his eyes affirmed the fact that rap music does have a possessive effect on its listener.

As he pulled into the parking lot of the BP convenience store, Damien turned the volume down on the car stereo. He didn't want EVERYONE to think that he wasn't civilized. He got out, locked the doors with the keyless remote, and entered the store to locate the beer section. He was surprised by the variety of provisions available in the modest building, and perused the isles to get a feel for what was offered, just in case he had to make a midnight run. There was a snack isle, bread isle, bait isle, and souvenir section in the far corner of the store. At the cash register, three stringy-haired white women whispered to each other quietly, while watching his every move with suspicion.

It was the first time Damien felt this uncomfortable since going into a beauty supply store on North Hairston a few months ago in Atlanta. That time, an Asian clerk followed Damien around like he was a rock star, except he wasn't looking for autographs. He started to cuss the clerk out, but he kept his cool. He brought his Pro-Line moisturizer, jumped into his BMW Z3, and peeled out of the parking lot, angry that folks would judge his intentions because of the color of his skin.

After retrieving three six-packs from the freezer, Damien turned around and headed back towards the front to pay for his purchase. Walking towards him were two co-eds wearing college paraphernalia. The tanned skin of the girl on the right intrigued Damien, and the short haircut she sported accentuated her bright smile as she made eye contact with him.

"Hi, ladies," Damien said, as he slowed his approach.

"Hello," they responded in unison, as they visually evaluated Damien's physique. He stood about 5'10 and weighed approximately 175 pounds. He wasn't the most muscular man in the world, but his two-inch sideburns, wavy hair, clean white teeth, and fair-skinned model face fed the playboy persona that he used as his bait. The girl he was attracted to turned to the side, bent down to grab a loaf of bread from the bottom shelf, and exposed the letters FSU, which were written in large, garnet letters across the behind of her gray shorts. Damien wasn't about to let the opportunity slide by, so he put on the full-court press.

"Your boyfriends must be crazy to allow you two pretty girls out in public alone. I'd have you two on a string twenty-four seven, eight days a week." He was really referring to the girl on the right. The girl on the left was slightly pudgy, but he knew how to run game.

"Thanks for the compliment," the friend said, as she continued to scope Damien like a zoo animal. Damien wasn't about to let this opportunity go, so he pressed on.

"Are you all here for the day, or did you rent a beach house?"

"My father has a timeshare here, so we came to relax after finals," the friend said.

"What about you?" she asked Damien.

"I'm here for the weekend with some co-workers. Our boss has a friend with a timeshare, so it's part-business, part-pleasure."

"I see," the pudgy girl said, obviously trying to block Damien's advance on her friend and make him focus on her warped body instead.

"Name's Damien, and yours?" Damien extended his hand cordially to formally introduce himself.

"I'm Brooke," the friend said. "And I'm Cindy," the brunette said, as she stood erect to reveal her luscious C-cups.

"You guys have something planned for the night?" Damien asked, wanting to know if he could supplement their entertainment.

"Well, we are kind of undecided right know," Cindy said, "but our two girlfriends were talking about going to the pizza parlor tonight to drink some beer and play the trivia game."

"Oh, really. Around what time?"

"Probably between eight-thirty and nine. We're going to the park to lay out in a little while."

"Mind if I meet you there tonight?"

The two girls looked at each other briefly, and then answered.

"No, no, we don't mind," Cindy said, as she looked Damien square in the eyes. In her opinion, he looked trustworthy. Plus, he was kinda cute. Damien wrote down Cindy's cell phone number, said goodbye, and walked to the front to pay for his items.

*   *   *

Stacey opened the sliding glass door, and re-entered the living area of the beach house. She held her hair magazine in one hand, and a half-empty glass of water in the other. She was wearing crème-colored sash Capri's with a blue sleeveless fitted v-neck shirt, and natural thong sandals. It wasn't the outfit Kelvin saw in his daydream, but it was just as appealing.

"So, where are you from?" Kelvin said.

"Shreveport. That's in Louisiana."

"Oh, I know where that is. We have several dealerships on our order list from there."

"You deal with cars?" Stacey asked, trying to act interested.

"Yeah, I work for Ford. I'm the production supervisor on my line. I make sure all the parts that are supposed to be on the cars get onto the cars."

"Oh, okay."

"Enough about me though; you know how to speak some Cajun?" Kelvin asked, trying to pick Stacey for background information.

"A little bit," she responded, not really wanting to be put on the spot.

"Speak it girl, say something!" Kelvin said in a demanding tone. He was trying to get her to maneuver her sexy lips with a foreign exchange of information.

"All right, one sentence. But after that, that's it, okay?"

"Fine, come with it."

"Cila qui rit vendredi va pleure dimanche."

"Daaiimm…" Kelvin said, as her beautiful, unintelligible sentence floated past his ears. "What's that mean?"

"It means, "He who laughs on Friday will cry on Sunday." Stacey explained, as she melted Kelvin with her doe-like eyes.

"Well, I wanna cry EVERY Sunday then," Kelvin said with a light chuckle. In his mind, he was thinking how he didn't want this weekend to end.

Leslie flushed, washed her hands, and returned to the living area to join Kelvin and Stacey.

"Excuse me for interrupting, but I have something I need to ask."

Stacey and Kelvin turned their attention towards Leslie, who cast a somber look on her round, chocolate face.

"Stacey, do you think I was being too hard on Kym today?"

Leslie felt guilty for accosting her co-worker, but had mixed feelings about apologizing.

"Leslie," Stacey said, as she placed her magazine and water glass on the L-part of the kitchen counter. "I personally feel the same way you do sometimes about people using their background to their advantage, but then again, don't we all?"

"What do you mean?" Leslie asked, as she sat down on the cloth love seat next to the counter.

"I mean men do it, women do it, blacks do it, whites do it, people in frats and sororities do it, even family members do it."

"Yeah," Kelvin added, "it's called nepotism. There was a lot of that going on in the auto industry up until the late-nineties. A lot of lawsuits were filed, and the manufacturers got tired of wasting their money settling cases, so they just changed the rules. I couldn't get one of my brothers a job at the plant if I tried. They still do it on the sales lots, but that's on them. You know, like the "good-ol' boy" network."

It was the first time since Leslie started working at Concepts that she showed any signs of weakness. Even though she meant what she said, she felt remorse for stooping so low in front of her co-workers. She always tried her best to mask her inner-feelings at work, because she knew that ethnic pride on the job would result in a short career. It was the same kind of outburst that cost Cynthia McKinney her job as a U.S. Congresswoman a few years back.

"So do you think I owe her an apology?" Leslie asked Stacey. She twiddled her thumbs together nervously.

"I don't know. But if I were you girl, I would seriously consider brushing up my resume. If Kym goes back to Logan with this, you might be in trouble. Remember the last employee meeting we had?"

"Yes; and?"

"They showed us a PowerPoint presentation that outlined the unemployment rates in the country. They said it would cause us to have to implement new marketing and advertising strategies, but it seems to me like they might have been saying something else."

"You know what?" Kelvin said, "Just apologize to her and get it over with. I have people up under me who try to get flip from time-to-time. They know who the man is, though. I've got fifteen people on my shifts that have paychecks that depend on my signature. It don't take much to fire a man, but it takes a whole lot to hire one, train him, and keep production up to par. If you bring a lot to the table, you probably don't have to worry about losing your job. Just make sure you swallow your pride, explain to her why you went off like that, and don't do it again. It'll make you a better person, too."

Leslie knew they were telling the truth, but she still harbored ill feelings about Kym. Her pride was her crutch. It always had been. That's probably the reason why she couldn't bring herself to conform to "corporate" standards during her internship. That's what led her back to Chicago and to her parent's house. Luckily for her, they knew someone at the *Defender* who hooked her up with her first marketing gig. She felt real comfortable there. She could be herself. She even wore natural twists until she moved to Atlanta, and had an Eldridge Cleaver poster hanging from her cubicle wall.

If it weren't for a torn relationship, she might still be in Chicago with Malik. But there was no way she was going to marry a man who suddenly expected her to be submissive in every aspect of her life, and used physical domination to enforce it. He justified it through his newfound Islamic faith. She eventually renounced it through her staunch feminine beliefs. Her mother taught her that. Angela wouldn't have it, Sojourner wouldn't have it, Mary McLeod wouldn't have it, and neither would Maya Angelou. Ironically, Leslie later found out on the Internet that Jimmie's Muslim name meant "master." If she had known that earlier, she thought, she never would have allowed herself to become his slave.

"Thanks guys, I really appreciate your opinion," Leslie said.

"No problem," said Stacey.

"Anytime," Kelvin said.

It was the first time that Stacey had seen a look of concern on Leslie's face. Although they were never close friends, they were cordial at work, and ate lunch together in the employee cafeteria from time to time. She always seemed so strong, so sure of herself. Stacey could tell that she was worried.

Kelvin excused himself, and went back out to the deck to try and rectify his culinary disaster. He cleaned out the wet charcoals, replaced them with new ones, and lit the new pile with determined concentration. *I'm not messing this one up,* he thought to himself. He opened the vent again, but only halfway, and waited a few minutes for the fire to simmer down. He decided to let the charcoals burn longer this time prior to cooking the food, so he asked Leslie and Stacey if they would baby-sit while he checked on Felicia. He hoped she wasn't super pissed off, just a little. If she was just a little pissed off, he knew he could light his wide smile on her and peck her on the check a few times. He could tell her he was sorry, that she was his queen, and everything would be okay again.

When he opened the door, he was surprised to find Felicia in the bathroom mirror with nothing on except her bra and panties. She was clutching her stomach pouch on both sides, with a few tears running down her face.

"Baby, what in the hell are you doing?" Kelvin said.

Felicia said nothing. She just turned from the mirror and grasped Kelvin in a big gorilla hug. She held him tight, and her tears became a stream. Her light boo-hoos had Kelvin asking himself what was wrong with his lady.

"Felicia, what's wrong? Look, I apologize about what happened on the deck. I didn't mean anything by it. What's up? Talk to me, c'mon."

Kelvin placed his hands on Felicia's face, and gently brought her off of his chest to reveal her teary eyes. In a slightly trembling voice, Felicia told Kelvin why she was hurting.

"I...I just want to feel wanted," she started out. "A...and it seems like since I had Jordan, you just don't pay me the same kind of attention you used to."

Felicia was half the woman she was during the meeting. Her lower eyelids were swollen, and Kelvin could feel her pain. He knew she was telling the truth, too. Ever since Jordan was born, it seemed to Kelvin that Felicia didn't WANT to be bothered with his attention. She was so busy being a mom, going to school, singing in the choir, and reading books that Kelvin often felt left out. That's why he started hanging out with his boys at Ford more, going to the strip clubs, and hanging out at Falcons games on Sundays.

He clutched Felicia tight, and bared his soul to the woman he loved.

"Baby, I love you more than anything on this planet." His tough heart suddenly felt soft. His body ached with emotion. It was one of those moments that you don't share with the fellas.

"I just want you to be happy," he continued. "Whatever I need to do, just let me know. You're beautiful to me, Felicia. I don't care about a little stomach. You're the woman I chose to marry, and I will love you until the day I die. When we get back to Atlanta, we're gonna take some time for ourselves. We need that. We're gonna get reunited, just like Peaches & Herb."

Felicia broke down even more, and Kelvin's eyes began to water. He grabbed his queen by the edge of her shoulders, lifted her up, and embraced her for what seemed like an eternity.

As they rocked back and forth, Kelvin kissed Felicia on the neck, and whispered something in her ear that he knew would get her to laugh.

"Now I know that stomach pouch is callin' a Kelvin Burger girl, so you'd better let me get back to the grill before it runs off your body and grows a mouth! It'll be runnin' up talkin' 'bout "Kelvin, I'm hungry!! Fix me one of those hot dogs, and a hamburger too!" His voice was in a high shrill, making him sound like an old lady.

Felicia's teary face immediately became a laugh factory. She wiped away the remaining moisture with her hands, and washed her face. Kelvin was glad that he could finally express to her what he longed to say, without a big blow-up argument. Everything was kosher. They were cool. But the grill was hot. Kelvin snapped to his senses, and excused himself to go check on the coals that were being babysat by Stacey and Leslie.

*   *   *

Damien pulled up into the driveway, and parked next to Kelvin's Expedition. He admired the shiny Sporza Lux rims that adorned the truck's fat black wall tires. He stepped out of the car, grabbed the brown paper bags from off the back seat, closed the door, and pushed the security button on the car's keyless entry device to lock the doors.

He walked up the steps, and approached the beach house. He noticed the name of it nailed to the wall to the right of the door: "The Tempest." He had been too busy when they first arrived to notice the sign. Stacey had him carrying her heavy-ass bags from the car. He felt like she did it on purpose, but he did it anyway, out of respect for everyone else. He remembered that word from the pocket dictionary he studied with while in college. It meant "a violent storm." *Fitting,* he thought to himself. That is what he had just witnessed between Kym and Leslie. He just hoped that the rest of the weekend wouldn't end up the same way.

Felicia opened the door for Damien, and went back into her room to finish preparing herself to look presentable. Damien walked into the kitchen, placed the paper bags on the counter, and looked up to see Kelvin coming through the glass sliding door.

"All right, man! We're ready to get this party started now chief!" Kelvin gave Damien some dap, and invited him out on the deck to join Leslie and Stacey, while he put the finishing touches on the grilled food.

Felicia exited the room and headed towards the deck to enjoy some of her husband's cooking. She glanced at the brown clock on her way outside. It read 4:47. Kym was beginning to stir as well. She could have slept all day after the morning she had. But her nose's sensory warning signals wouldn't allow her to sleep past the smell of Kelvin's barbeque session. She was still thoroughly embarrassed by the ethnic escapade during the meeting, and was seriously contemplating an early return trip via the nearest rental car agency. However, she remembered that she and Felicia were directly responsible for the marketing plan that they were creating. She swallowed her pride, got out of bed, and put on some comfortable clothes so she could join in on the barbeque fest.

Antoine was still fast asleep. They decided not to bother him, and put a plate to the side for when he got up. Felicia led the grace, and everyone made plates for themselves. Hamburgers, hot dogs, coleslaw, and BBQ baked beans. *I wonder why good southern food always makes you fart*, Leslie thought to herself, as she scooped another spoonful of beans into her mouth.

Leslie loved to eat, and snack, too. That's how she handled pressure situations. That's why she weighed almost 170 pounds. That was bad, considering she stood just 5'5. She weighed 127 when she graduated from Hampton.

After she moved back to Chicago, her mom insisted that she eat more. She was tired of Leslie trying to keep up with the models and actresses by eating fruit and salads. Malik only made it worse. He started calling her fat as part of his mental control plan. He watched her gain over twenty pounds in less than a year. A few more had been added since then. But right now, that didn't matter. She really wanted to apologize to Kym for going off on her earlier during the meeting.

Kym was sitting in one of the lounge chairs finishing her meal. The topic of conversation was the beach and how beautiful it was. Small talk. But she participated anyway, so she wouldn't alienate herself from the group. Kym looked up, and felt her heart race as Leslie pulled up next to her and sat in a lounge chair. She didn't know whether to expect an apology, or a good-ol' fashioned beat down. She kept her composure, however, and flashed a cordial smile at her famed accuser.

Leslie added a few more words to the beach conversation, and turned to her left to face Kym. Kym eyed Leslie with suspicion, and listened as Leslie asked for forgiveness.

"Look Kym," Leslie said, "It was totally inappropriate to say what I said earlier…. It just seems like I can never get ahead, and sometimes I try to place the blame on other people. I know I hurt your feelings, but I really hope you can find the strength to accept my apology. What I said was out of order, ignorant, and just plain wrong."

Leslie's words were slow and deliberate, a sure sign that she meant what she said. Kym looked at Leslie for a few moments, and voiced her response.

"What you said really hurt me. I've never felt so embarrassed in my life. I also felt undermined. As the manager over this project, I felt like you tried to conduct a power play. I am willing to accept your apology. However, I still may have to report this to Logan and have a written reprimand placed in your personnel file. I just have to think about it, okay?"

Damien, Stacey, Felicia, and Kelvin were faking their conversation. All ears were on Kym and Leslie. After they finished eating, Kelvin went downstairs to wait for Damien to play some pool. The ladies cleaned up outside, and headed back into the beach house to relax in the A.C.

*   *   *

5 Friday Evening

"Rack 'em up!" Kelvin exclaimed, as he anxiously awaited Damien's footsteps to turn the corner from upstairs.

"Damn bruh, you don't waste any time jumping on the racks do you?" Damien said.

He was right behind Kelvin, but Kelvin was so excited to finally be in his element, that he almost cart wheeled down the half-winding stairwell trying to reach the rec room.

Kelvin surveyed the 8-foot Oak Knight pool table as if he was a Spanish conquistador surveying a treasure map of the Aztec empire. With its chrome feet, red wine colored table carpet, and diamond/geographic lined patterns on its hips, it may as well have been a super model from Trinidad walking past a maximum-security prison yard.

Kelvin stared intensely at the way the silver triple-light fixture's chrome finish reflected onto the table's surface. It was almost as if the table was begging him to come and play.

"Hey, man!" Kelvin was jolted from his table lusting by Damien's loud, sarcastic yell.

"You can't play without a stick!" Damien laughed, as he tossed a stick to Kelvin and chalked the head of his. Kelvin did the same, and inquired about who would break the rack, trying to be the southern gentleman that he was raised to be.

The sight of the pool table sitting in the middle of a room with a spectacular view of the Gulf of Mexico skyline was too much for Kelvin to handle. He had never been to the beach. Not even Lake Lanier. His only exposure to outside water had been pay-for-fishing lakes in Decatur with his uncle Jake and two brothers, the Centennial Olympic Park fountains with Felicia and Jordan, and the water hose outside his momma's house when he was growing up during those hot, muggy Atlanta summers.

Kelvin had a suggestion. "Say man, let's pop a couple 'a brews before I commence to spanking your bee-hind on this table."

Damien let out a homeboy chuckle and slid to the mini-bar that was situated on the wall between the pool table and the stairwell.

"What's your preference?" Damien asked, as he flashed a cold, dripping right hand holding a Budweiser and a Michelob bottle over the mini-bar's countertop.

"I prefer one of those cold-ass Heinekens that you snuck down here with the rest of that watered down brew," Damien said laughing. He placed the Budweiser back into the Styrofoam cooler and dove in with his left hand for the Heineken.

"Whooo-ooh!" Damien exclaimed, opening his lungs to express the pain he felt while dipping into the Arctic freeze. He retreated with his intended target, placed it on the counter next to his 12-ounce victim, and dried his hands off with a towel.

"Kelvin, you're trying to set me up for a loss, bruh. I can't play with my hands feeling like ice, ice, baby!"

The two busted out in an uncontrollable laugh that made the women upstairs wonder what was going on.

"Are you all okay?" Felicia yelled from the top of the stairwell.

"Yeah, we're straight," Kelvin yelled back in a loud, bellowing voice, sounding more like a teenager than a thirty-three year old man.

All of their testosterone-laced excitement and commotion had broken Antoine's late afternoon slumber.

He opened his door, which sat cattycorner to the pool table from bar's view, and gave the two comrades a disgusting look.

"Look, can you guys hold it down? I'm trying to get some sleep."

Kelvin seized the moment and threw a snide insult at him, a return volley from this morning. "Aww, Antoine, I thought you were going to join the boys and help us make MORE noise down here."

Damien chimed in. "You might as well wake up, 'Toine. You get away from your lady and the boss for a weekend, and you want to sleep. Shake the cobwebs off and join the fellas."

Antoine was contemplating whether to cuss them out or take them up on the offer. After a few moments of reflection, he chose the latter.

"All right, you idiots. Let me brush my teeth and put on some shorts. I'll be out in a minute."

Antoine closed his door, mumbled a few improprieties, and changed out of his linen, herringbone-colored Calvin Klein lounge outfit into a baby blue and white Kenneth Cole polo shirt with khaki shorts. He grabbed his Oral-B electric toothbrush, Rejuvenating Effects toothpaste, a pack of Listerine breath strips, slid on a pair of Cole Haan travel slippers and headed towards the pool table, making a right into the mini-hallway that led towards the bathroom adjacent to Leslie's sleeping quarters.

Antoine couldn't help but notice the framed print hanging at the end of the hallway. As he prepared to make a left into the small guest bathroom, he absorbed the sight of two middle-aged white men wearing brown Kangols and old-school plaid parachute pants. They were standing on a golf course conversing with a hand on one hip and the other supporting their clubs, which were planted squarely on the ground.

To their right stood a black caddie, who looked to be about fifty years old, with his shoulders slumped over a bag of clubs. He was baring his teeth, doing his best impersonation of a 1930's Sambo.

* * *

"Let's flip for it!" Damien said. He was getting warmed up, especially after downing a few gulps of his brew. He placed his bottle back onto the counter and reached into his pocket to retrieve some change. He pulled out a nice, shiny Georgia quarter and tossed it around in his hand.

Kelvin stopped breast-feeding on his Heineken long enough to utter a response. "Alright, but you know I'm old school, so let's put a friendly wager on our game."

"Alright, bet," Damien responded, sounding determined not to back down to Kelvin's challenge. "What's the wager?"

Kelvin sized Damien up with his eyes, and then put his terms out there.

"The loser has to play Chef Boyardee in the morning. I'm talking full course and all of the food groups, not Continental."

Damien let out a loud chuckle and responded confidently.

"You're on, partna!" The two dapped each other up, and Damien handed the coin over to Antoine, who had just returned from the bathroom.

"Here, flip it," Damien said, as he took one last swig from his brew.

Antoine took the coin reluctantly, positioned it in his right hand between his thumb and forefinger, and let it fly into the air above the table. After a few blurry revolutions, it landed on the table, bounced around, and finally rested on its back.

"Heads!" Damien exclaimed. He racked up the brand-new balls, and let them fly with a crack of his stick on the white ball.

After fifteen minutes of plotting and prodding, Damien confidently blasted the black eight ball into the right corner pocket from two and a half feet away.

"Yeah!" Damien yelled out. "That's what I'm talkin' about! I like mine scrambled well, bacon done, toast brown with jelly, and grits thick with lots of butter. I'll put the seasoning salt on myself."

The three burst out with laughter, and Kelvin reset the rack. For the next twenty minutes, he pummeled Antoine into submission, leaving five of his striped balls on the table when victory was claimed.

"You wanna run that back pretty boy?" Kelvin was ready to show Damien how it was REALLY done in the Deck.

After being dragged out to all of the local cocktail lounges as an under-aged minor by his uncle and older brothers, Kelvin was more than equipped to strap on the pool stick and run game on the silly marks who didn't realize a con when they saw one. Uncle Jake had taught him the rules. Rule number one in the gambling game was to always let your opponent win the first game. Get him comfortable. Then raise the stakes. Kelvin was ready to get paid.

"How 'bout some chump change to make the game a little more interesting. Let's say twenty dollars?" Kelvin said. He spread his wings halfway, opened his palms, and lightly shrugged his shoulders to give a nonchalant effect.

"That IS chump change. Is that all you've got?" Damien's deliberate response elicited an immediate counter-response from Kelvin.

"Okay big money, double and a half. Let's bust it for fifty."

Damien had been around the block too. His dad was famous for running small-time scams back in Cleveland. When he wasn't locked up or out hustling, he was tutoring his son on how to hustle. At the top of the list: when to play and when to fold. Damien learned to recognize the player before he recognized the game. And Kelvin was definitely a player. Plus, Damien had something better to get into.

"I tell you what. When I get back tonight from exploring the island, I just might take you up on your offer. Otherwise, I'll see you at breakfast honey," Damien said.

Kelvin's angry response was predictable. "Alright, be a punk. But if you come back late, expect toast and orange juice."

Antoine, who was getting tired of their macho standoff, started walking towards the stairwell towards some intelligent conversation.

"You want some more before you leave?" Kelvin said. He wasn't quite ready to put his cue stick to sleep.

"No sir," Antoine replied. In his mind, he was calling them both buffoons. Plus, Christian men are not supposed to gamble.

Damien retired his cue stick, and went into his room to change. He opened the sliding glass window, cut on the medium sized television that sat on his dresser, plopped down on the bed, and gazed at the amber horizon that loomed across the Gulf.

He admired the way the waves pounded the shoreline. He listened to the seagulls play their final selections for the evening. He liked the tall blades of grass that belly-danced in twenty directions as if they were convulsing to the whispers of the ocean breeze that whipped along the island's front door. Most of all, he admired the smell of the salty Gulf. He closed his eyes, laid his head back, and took a deep breath. Yes, the smell of salt turned him on. It was the smell he lived for, each and every day. It was the smell of a woman. Not her perfume or her breath, but her essence. And he had to have it. All the time. On his mouth, on his body, or in hers. It didn't matter. He was addicted.

Damien reached into his pocket and pulled out Cindy's number that he had scribbled on a piece of paper from his convenience store trip earlier in the day. It was ten digits long. The first three numbers read 850. Long distance. He reached over the side of the bed and rummaged through the side pocket of his black travel bag, and grabbed a calling card. His prepaid cellular minutes were busted last week. He glanced at his watch, picked up the phone, and dialed.

*   *   *

Upstairs, a rambunctious debate on gender differences had everyone in a pleasant uproar. By the time Kelvin and Antoine arrived, the conversation was centered on the chemistry of male behavior. Stacey said that men were like trained circus animals. Keep feeding them sexual treats, she said, and they will stay happy. Leslie stated that men are a bunch of power-mongering cavemen dressed for the 21st Century. Men wouldn't survive without women to stroke their egos, she said. Felicia talked about men having to run in packs to feel important. Kym said men were jealous that they weren't born women. Women enjoyed the luxuries of better shopping, better physical assets, and multiple orgasms, she said. The men were eager to give their input.

"I think women put on a front towards men until they find their "prince in shining armor," Antoine said, making quotation marks with his fingers. "They're looking for financial security, a stable religious environment, and a complete physical package. Basically, somebody like me."

The reaction from the females was swift. After a brief chorus of "Aww Pleases," Leslie spoke up.

"See what I mean? You've been getting your ego stroked. Just because you wear a little designer clothing and just got engaged does not make you God's gift to the world. Your fiancée doesn't love you just because you've got a decent job, either. She could've easily gotten with a baller or dated outside of her race. Lord knows we're putting out some sorry black men these days."

A number of sounds came out of the female section. "Umm Humm, Tell it girl!" It sounded like an old tent revival. Kelvin didn't agree with Antoine's egotistical comment, but right now it was them versus the women, and Antoine needed some backup.

"If it wasn't for men," Kelvin said, "women wouldn't have anywhere to sleep. Where would they shop? Last time I checked, men built the malls. Cars too. As a matter of fact, where would you go visit? What plane would you ride?"

Felicia shot back. "Please, Kelvin, the only reason women haven't built things like men have is because we've been too busy taking care of your kids!" Catcalls and laughter erupted from the women. She continued, as a call and response session initiated.

"And when we haven't been doing that, we've been cooking,"

"Uh, huh,"

"Cleaning,"

"Say it, girl!"

"And washing your DOGGONE dirty clothes when you come home from playing outside in the dirt!" The ladies exploded with more emotion, exchanging high-fives and high-pitched shrills.

The men were defeated. Felicia hit a soft spot in Kelvin and Antoine's heart. All they could do was laugh. Because even though women now enjoy many of the same career opportunities as men, they didn't a generation ago. Kelvin's mom Gloria raised him and his two older brothers the best way she could. When she took disability after being diagnosed with Diabetes, the only things she could do were the things Felicia had just named.

Same with Antoine. His granny was a retired educator, and kept their house immaculate. His house was the house where everybody in the neighborhood wanted to hang out at, especially for Sunday dinner. That's why Antoine was so devastated to lose both of his grandparents within two years of each other. They had raised him like he was their own child. So it hurt even more when he found out that he had been adopted from foster care when he was three. They didn't tell him, because they wanted him to have as normal a childhood as possible. He didn't find out until he and the family lawyer went over their wills, and was told that they had set up a $150,000 trust fund for him. But that didn't matter now. He was about to start a real family of his own.

6 Friday Evening

Felicia suggested that they play a game of Taboo as a formal icebreaker. Even though everyone was familiar with each other as co-workers, they had never enjoyed much personal interaction. Plus, she wanted Kelvin to feel part of the group. She saw him talking with Damien, and observed his interactions with Stacey, but she knew he felt uncomfortable about coming this weekend. She insisted, however, because she didn't want him to think she was coming down here just to party with her co-workers, especially Damien and Antoine.

Damien walked upstairs after preparing for the evening, and joined Kelvin and Antoine as teammates. Felicia was the timekeeper, scorekeeper, and referee in case of a dispute. After about forty minutes, the ladies were almost seven points ahead of the guys, and Antoine was getting frustrated with Kelvin. He was having difficulty with some of the answers, because they were unfamiliar to his brain's dictionary.

Kelvin was feeling frustrated too. *How do you come up with a clue for the word Beatnik?* he thought to himself. Coming up with answers was just as difficult. When Damien pulled the word "Confucius," his first verbal clue was Fortune Cookie. All Kelvin could think of was fried rice and chicken wings. Luckily, Damien was able to lead Antoine to that answer.

After the ladies took their turn, it was on Kelvin. He waited for Felicia's signal, and pulled. The word "Scurry" wasn't even in his vocabulary, but the forbidden words on the card gave him a hint of what to say. He couldn't say run or move, so he said "dip fast, do like a mouse." He pumped his arms like he was running, hoping that Damien or Antoine would catch on. Had he been familiar with the corporate culture, he could have said, "Name a character from the book *Who Moved My Cheese*." Frustrated, he passed to the next card. After one minute, Felicia mashed the sick-sounding turquoise and pink buzzer and tallied up the score: thirty-six points for the women, twenty-five for the men.

"Are you guys ready to give up?" Felicia asked.

"Hell yeah, Kelvin responded."

Felicia gave him the "you-don't-have-to-be-macho-and-ignorant-too, look." A disgusted Antoine agreed. Damien was on a mission anyway, so he was eager to fold.

"We enjoyed beating you guys," Stacey remarked, with a sly grin.

"Same here," added Leslie. Kym's smile did all of her talking. Damien glanced at his chrome wristwatch. It read 8:39.

"Anybody want some pizza?" He said.

"No, I'm still full from the barbeque," Stacey said.

"Me, too," said Kym and Felicia.

Antoine had eaten prior to playing Taboo. He declined as well. Kelvin and Leslie told Damien to bring an extra pizza back just in case. Damien said goodbye, and floated into the night breeze.

Kym excused herself into the bedroom. She was tired, and needed some sleep. Stacey borrowed Antoine's laptop to check her website hits and respond to some e-mails. Kelvin invited Felicia to an evening walk on the secluded beach. She happily agreed. Antoine needed to check on his fiancée, so he excused himself into the sitting room so he could get better service on his cell phone.

Antoine plopped down on the non-descript blue sofa and turned around to peek out of the front window. Damien was backing out in the Taurus and caught Antoine's stare. Antoine let go of the blinds, turned around, and dialed.

"Hello?" It was Shauna.

"Hey baby, this is Antoine."

"I know who this is."

"What are you doing?"

"Nothing, me and some of the girls had Bible study this evening, and decided to catch some jazz and a little dinner afterwards."

Antoine could hear the ambiance of a restaurant in the background, as dishes clinked and musical notes floated from a jazz ensemble.

"It's getting late, which side of town are you on?"

"I'm at C'est Bon."

Her response was curt, and Antoine could sense an attitude. He refrained from asking her what she was still doing on the Eastside. Bible study was usually held on Wednesdays at Wings of Grace Baptist, where they worshipped. That was in Stone Mountain, but members lived all over Metro Atlanta.

"What's wrong, baby? Was everything alright at work?"

"Yeah. I just have a slight headache, that's all. I'll be okay though."

"Are you sure?"

"Yes, I'm sure."

"Okay, well I guess I'll let you go."

"Okay."

"I love you, baby."

"I love you too."

"Bye."

"Okay, bye."

Shauna pressed the end button on her cell phone and exhaled a deep breath. She was having a difficult time trying to figure out how she was going to tell Trevor that their secret relationship had to end. Up until now, their little indiscretions had been a game. All this time, she had Antoine thinking that Trevor was her cousin. He even helped her move into Antoine's new house. She didn't want to cross the altar with a dark cloud hanging over her conscience, but she had feelings for Trevor. She knew this wouldn't be easy.

Trevor came into sight as he returned from the restroom. Shauna marveled at his chiseled 6'2 frame and his chocolate baldhead. He always looked good, she thought, but tonight he looked exceptionally well. He was wearing a dark-brown Fubu Suit with a thin crème colored pullover shirt, and Bacco Bucci dress shoes. His M7 cologne emitted a masculine scent that made her want to forget that she was engaged. He had invited her here for his birthday. She reluctantly accepted.

Trevor was lusting after Shauna as well. When she first walked into the lobby, he had to bite his bottom lip to keep from jumping her right in front of everyone. She was wearing a strapless black knee-length dress that was low-cut to expose the top of her breasts. Her hair was pinned up in a bun, and she sported an eight-row crystal choker that Antoine brought her for Valentine's Day. Her perfume was sweet and sensual, and the heels that she wore boosted her 5'6 frame and extra three or four inches. After finishing an appetizer, Trevor was ready to leave the restaurant.

"Hey baby, you back?" Shauna asked, as Trevor took his seat near the large windows.

"Yeah. Did you order yet?"

"No, I got a phone call from—"

Trevor reached over and placed his index finger over Shauna's lip.

"Shhh… Not tonight. I don't want to discuss any problems you're having with your man. Tonight I just want to enjoy you, okay?"

Shauna shook her head yes as she gazed into his penetrating brown eyes. She caressed her bottom lip with her tongue and felt butterflies scatter in her stomach.

They had been playing this game for almost two years now. They might have been husband and wife, but for the fact that Trevor was already married. Shauna wouldn't have given him her number at Publix if she had known. But it was too late to turn back once she caught him in his lies. She was hooked.

"Have you all decided on your main course, or would you like a few suggestions?" the polite waitress asked, as she refilled Shauna's glass with red wine.

"No thanks," Trevor replied. "I'll take the check now. The appetizer was just fine."

"Okay sir, I'll be right back." The waitress walked off, and Trevor turned his focus back to Shauna. He wanted to grab her hands, but didn't want to draw any unwanted attention.

"Shauna, I know you're getting married soon, and lately I've been sensing your uneasiness with this relationship," he said.

"I don't want our selfishness to destroy what we have at home, so I think tonight should be the last time we see each other." Trevor's mood had suddenly become serious. He spoke from the heart, and hoped that Shauna would be able to handle it coming like this.

"Trevor," Shauna said, looking directly into Trevor's soul. "What we have is wrong, but it feels so right. All I've ever wanted was a man who is as compassionate and loving as you are.

I feel as if you were destined to be a part of my life. But if we have to stop seeing each other, just promise that you'll never forget the time we spent together. Promise that you'll hold a spot in your heart for me. And promise, Trevor, that you will understand that we can never, ever tell anyone about this relationship, okay?"

Trevor nodded in agreement, and paid cash for the bill. He stood up from his chair, adjusted his jacket, and escorted Shauna towards the front door exit. Once they were outside, Trevor gently grabbed Shauna's left pinkie finger and led her to the side of the building. The energy of the streetlight that stood across from them cast their long, dark silhouettes across the parking lot. Trevor pulled Shauna close, and spoke softly into her ear.

"Baby, just one more time."

Shauna's eyes moistened, as she contemplated not seeing him again. She looked down, and then up into his eyes. Her body language said all that he needed to know. Her hands trembled, as he led her to the La Quinta hotel behind the restaurant. They walked through the lobby, and rode up on the elevator to their favorite room. For the next two hours, a "Do Not Disturb" sign stood guard to the most intense lovemaking session they had ever experienced in their life.

*   *   *

Kelvin and Felicia paused on the deck for a few minutes and held each other tight while the night breeze whistled past their standing lane. They talked about how good it felt to be away from home for a little while, and how good the fresh, salty air smelled compared to the carbon-monoxide cocktail being brewed daily by Atlanta's commuters and factories. They walked down the deck walkway, and listened as the blades of beach grass brushed gently against the wooden planks.

They walked out onto the beach, and felt the sugary-white sand crush under their sandals and make squeaking noises. Kelvin laughed, as Felicia lost her balance on the soft confection. The bright moonlight cast just enough light to illuminate the nightlife of the beach's fauna. Tiny birds scampered across the wet sand, trying to avoid the rushing water that rolled onto the beach. Tiny Sand and Hermit Crabs played peek-a-boo with their human guests, disappearing and reappearing within seconds of their arrival and departure. Kelvin stooped down a few times to retrieve broken shells that he could use as souvenirs for his co-workers at Ford.

Their daily problems temporarily went unnoticed, as the secluded stretch of nature serenaded the couple with its sights and sounds. Kelvin let Felicia's hand go and removed his sandals. He hopped sideways into the rolling tide, and felt the sand disappear under his feet each time a wave was sucked back into the Gulf. Felicia's thoughts suddenly turned to Jordan.

"Oh, goodness."

"What," Kelvin said, wondering what Felicia was talking about.

"Did you call Jordan today?"

"Nah, did you?"

"No, I forgot. I told him that we would call every night before he went to bed."

"Felicia, let that boy grow up. He's almost five and he has a god-brother to play with. Anyway, you know Apreal is taking good care of that boy."

"I know baby, but I promised him I would call."

"Okay, worry monster. But tomorrow you owe me another walk. This time longer, okay?"

Felicia agreed, and they made a u-turn and headed back towards the house.

While Kelvin and Felicia enjoyed their walk on the beach, Stacey and Antoine decided to compare college experiences. Antoine rolled up his right shirtsleeve to reveal the tattoo he received as a member of the FAMU "Marching 100" and Kappa Kappa Psi. Stacey showed Antoine a burn she received on her left wrist while rushing to iron her clothes for a party. They playfully argued about who had the best school, FAMU or Clark-Atlanta. Antoine won hands-down. Stacey couldn't name two famous alumni of her school. Antoine named ten: Common,

Willie Galimore, Althea Gibson, Carrie Meek, Bob Hayes, Pam Oliver, Marquis Grissom, Vince Coleman, Lasalle D. Lefall, and Kwame Kilpatrick. He didn't have to mention the band; she already knew. She told him that he couldn't use the Marching 100 because that was an organization. He said he didn't care.

*   *   *

7 Friday Night

Kelvin and Felicia opened the sliding glass door on the top deck, and entered the living area out of breath. They had run the entire length of the deck walkway like two little kids, racing to see who would win. Kelvin was laughing so hard that he stopped ten feet behind Felicia as they closed in on the finish line. But he didn't care. He was too busy enjoying himself, acting like an adolescent again, and enjoying his time away from the city. As they entered the beach house, Antoine and Stacey were just getting heated up with their HBCU politics.

"Who you got Stacey, who you got?" Antoine prodded, as Stacey sat dumbfounded at FAMU's alumni list.

"Nobody," Stacey responded, determined to put up a fight. "But WE'VE got the AU Center. We also have Atlanta. Name the clubs in Tallahassee."

Antoine thought long and hard. He had heard about two clubs that were jumping back in the day called Faces and Fahrenheit, but beyond that, the only club he could think of was Club Leisure, which was located downtown. Stacey began rattling off a list of clubs and venues in Atlanta, when Kelvin intervened.

"What ch'all talkin' 'bout?" he asked. Stacey told him, and Kelvin rose valiantly to her defense.

"Aww, c'mon Antoine," he said. "You know there ain't nothing going on in Florida except some Jam Pony mix tapes and Daytona Beach during Spring Break."

"I wouldn't know about that, partna," Antoine countered. "I don't do too much partying. Partying can get you caught up, cause you not to graduate, you know what I mean?"

Once again, Antoine had shot Kelvin an unnecessarily snide comment. This time, however, he said something specific that only he and Felicia knew about. She had to have been talking to him, Kelvin thought to himself. How else could Antoine know? Kelvin was in the process of completing his undergraduate degree online in business management at the University of Phoenix. He had dropped out of Albany State during his freshman year, after flunking two consecutive semesters. Too many parties did him in. It was hard as hell to make a ten o'clock class when you were drunk and didn't lie down until six in the morning.

Fortunately, his homeboys Bo and Jarell had the guts to stick it out. They both graduated on CP time and had decent jobs in the Albany area. Bo was the manager at the Holiday Inn. He hooked Kelvin and Felicia up with a free room, and gave Kym one at half-price, which Kelvin and Felicia paid for. Jarell was a social worker by profession, and moonlighted as a music promoter. He wanted Kelvin to stay the whole weekend so he could meet an underground Georgia rap group called The Crunk Boyz, but Kelvin had to decline.

Kelvin thought about Antoine's comment for a second, and responded in a firm, cordial manner.

"Yeah, I KNOW what you mean," Kelvin said. "It's like that sometimes."

*   *   *

Felicia walked into the master bedroom and picked up the phone. She dialed the eleven-digit number. A light female voice answered the phone.

"Hello?"

"Hey girl, this is Felicia."

"Girl, why are you calling here again? I told you yesterday that Jordan was okay. He and Michael have been playing all day. They ate pizza, took a bath an hour ago, and now they're watching *Stuart Little 2* in the family room."

"I know, I know. But girl, I told Jordan that I would call every day. I didn't want him to think that his mommy was abandoning him."

"Phew. Girrl, ANYWAY… Here he is. JORDANNN!" Apreal yelled Jordan's name, but he didn't answer.

"Hold on girl," Apreal said. She walked out of the kitchen, around the corner, and down the hallway to the family room. Jordan was fast asleep on the couch. Michael was stretched out on the floor, on top of a big Spongebob 3D pillow. She grabbed the remote control, and turned the DVD off. She decreased the volume and changed the channel to Smooth Jazz on the satellite guide. It had been a long weekend. Her husband Jeff was out of town on business, and she had the kids all to herself. Lately, she had been thinking about having another child, but after test-driving the idea, Apreal was having second thoughts. She walked back to the kitchen, grabbed the phone, and opened the refrigerator to pull out a cold bottle of wine.

"Felicia, Jordan is asleep," Apreal said in a low whisper.

"For real?"

"Yes, girl. I wish I had some film… this is definitely a Kodak moment."

Felicia breathed a deep sigh, and flashed a quiet smile, the kind only a mother knows. She told Apreal that she would call back in the morning, and hung up the phone. Kelvin opened the door, and headed towards the bathroom.

"Did you talk to him?"

"No, he was already asleep."

"I figured that. He probably played so hard that he couldn't stay awake if you paid him." Kelvin let out a slight chuckle and walked into the bathroom to brush his teeth and take a shower.

"You taking a shower?" Kelvin yelled out to Felicia from the bathroom as he adjusted the water to a comfortable temperature setting. Felicia stood up, dropped her dress, took off her bra, stepped out of her sandals, and headed for the bathroom to join her husband in the warm rainwater. Once in the shower, Kelvin lathered himself up, handed the soap to Felicia, and spoke to her about Antoine.

"Felicia, what's up with Antoine? That fool has been trippin' since he got here. I don't know nothin' about him except what you tell me, and that's too much information for anybody."

"I don't know, baby. Maybe he's just nervous about his wedding plans, and telling his future in-laws that he and Shauna are shacking until they get married."

Kelvin turned his body to rinse, and continued to prod Felicia for information.

"So how does Antoine know that I don't have my degree yet?"

Felicia gave Kelvin the "I-don't-have-a-clue-but-I-know-I-look-guilty" expression, and tried to do some explaining.

"Kelvin, Antoine doesn't talk to a lot of people at work, because he's saved now. There aren't many of us at work who are under the cross. Whenever he needs someone to talk to, I lend him an ear."

"And obviously, visa-versa." Kelvin added, trying to egg Felicia on.

"Look Kelvin, you're my husband. I would never say something about you to hurt you, especially to other people. If I mentioned that to him, it was probably because I was complaining about how busy we are sometimes. I was just telling him how glad I would be when we both finished school, that's all."

Felicia was ALMOST telling the truth. She complained, but it was about Kelvin not making enough money as he should down at Ford. In other words, she was complaining to Antoine about them being broke.

Kelvin eyed Felicia suspiciously, and moved to the back of the shower to allow Felicia to rinse.

"Alright, Felicia. But I'm telling you, I don't like the way he's coming at me with those slick-ass comments. He's got one more time to say something out of his place and I'm gonna show out on him."

Felicia knew Kelvin was telling the truth. Antoine was the kind of person that demanded attention. At work, Felicia was his sounding board. He talked to her about all of his problems, and gave her his undivided attention when necessary. They weren't attracted to each other sexually; it was more of a mental infatuation. They knew each other's business, and liked to feel as if they were there for one another when needed. There was a possibility that Antoine was feeling slightly jealous of Kelvin, because Felicia had been wrapped under him all day. Husband or not, Antoine was upset.

"Kelvin," Felicia pleaded. "Don't go showing off on him. He's going through a lot right now, and needs emotional support. And I'm sorry if he tried to embarrass you. I'll speak to him about it tomorrow."

"Whatever," Kelvin said, as he flexed his chest muscles one at a time to make them jump. Felicia turned the shower off, and pulled the towels from the shower bar so they could dry off. She kissed Kelvin on the lips and shoulder, and moved down to his chest, pausing to lick one of his nipples. Then, she went down further to the inside of his right hip, where she sucked a spot for a few seconds, leaving a red cherry next to his manhood. She knew how to deflect this negative conversation with Kelvin. It worked, too. His soldier jumped to full attention in no time flat, and Kelvin was eager to relieve the sexual tension that had suddenly built up in his second brain. He finished drying off, and imagined Felicia doing nasty things to his body. Felicia wasn't into having sex on a regular basis, but she knew what to do when it counted. As soon as Felicia finished brushing her teeth, Kelvin met her at the bathroom door with a facial grin like the *Mature Cat* commercial from back in the day.

"Come here, girl."

"What, boy?" Felicia countered, trying to play hard to get.

"You know what's up. Come over here to this bed and let me show you how King Kong gets down."

Felicia laughed, and told Kelvin to lock the door. She turned off the lights, and slid underneath the thick bedding. Kelvin grabbed her slender frame, climbed on, and entered her from the top. She squealed and moaned for the next twenty minutes as he grinded and pumped with all of his might. The intensity of their lovemaking did not escape unnoticed. Kym had to turn onto her side and put a pillow on her exposed ear to muffle Felicia's moans. After they both experienced intense orgasms, Kelvin rolled off and cradled Felicia's body from the side. They fell asleep within seconds.

Stacey and Antoine wrapped up their "best black school" debate, and said goodnight. Leslie was still awake downstairs. She had taken a bath, and was watching an old blaxsploitation flick she found on cable called *Black Samson*. She enjoyed these kinds of movies. To her, they represented a time and a place that no longer existed in black culture. She watched and waited, patiently anticipating Damien's return so she could eat some pizza. She hoped he would be returning soon. She was hungry.

*   *   *

Damien, Cindy, and her two friends walked out of B.J.'s Pizza, laughing like they had known each other for years. It probably had something to do with the two pitchers of beer they had just finished. Damien didn't care about the shocked look on some of the patron's faces when they saw him enjoying the company of four white girls. His goal for the weekend was to enjoy himself, and so far that's exactly what he was doing.

Damien put the pizza he ordered into the Taurus, and escorted the girls back to their car. He snuck a peek at his chrome wristwatch. It read 11:29. He wanted to ask Cindy to walk with him on the beach, but he knew Brooke would interfere. He decided to call it a night and get with her one-on-one tomorrow. He opened the doors of the Volkswagen for Brooke, Erica, and Michelle, and walked around the back to the driver's side to try and sell Cindy on a solo outing.

"Cindy, I had a great time with you all tonight. Thanks for the beer."

"No problem, we enjoyed you too."

"So, what are your plans for tomorrow?"

"I don't think we have too much planned. We may rent some scooters and explore the island, and then get drunk over there."

She was pointing towards the St. George Island Bistro. Damien looked too, and from the number of rebel flags and handkerchiefs he saw on the trucks and heads of their customers, he knew that would be too much for him.

"Why don't you call me when you come back in tomorrow evening, and maybe we can hang out."

"Okay, I'll do that."

Damien reached for the door, and opened it for Cindy so she could drive her intoxicated friends back to their beach house. He looked into her sexy eyes, scanned her bosom, and pulled her towards him for a hug. She patted him lightly on the back, climbed into her car, and drove off.

Damien stepped into the Taurus, put in a mixed jazz CD, and breezed down the road towards Paradise Lane. He parked, grabbed the pizza off the passenger's seat, and went upstairs to the front door. He knocked, but no one answered. He rang the doorbell; finally, Leslie walked upstairs to let him in.

"Damn girl," Damien said, "I was beginning to believe you didn't want any of this pizza."

"Yeah, yeah," Leslie responded. "Just bring that box around this corner to the kitchen so I can gain a few more pounds."

Damien was still hot and bothered from looking at Cindy's body, and needed a release. He wasn't attracted to Leslie, but his dad told him a long time ago that coochie didn't have a face. He didn't think she liked him either, but maybe she needed a release too. He knew why she left Chicago, and he also knew that she always complained about not having a man to cuddle up with at night. *This is going to have to be smooth,* he thought to himself. *I can't fuck this job up like the one in Charlotte. I don't need any more sexual harassment charges.* He gathered his courage, and let his inner-player work.

"Leslie, why are you always talking about yourself? There's nothing wrong with a thick woman. Where I'm from, skinny women don't get any play. It's too damn cold up there, especially during the holidays."

"Why thank you, Damien. I'll take that as a compliment, even though you know I know you're full of shit. I'm from Chi-town, and skinny girls get all the play up there too, so stop fronting."

Leslie sat on the loveseat, took a bite from one of the two slices of pizza that she held hostage, and gazed out into the midnight darkness. The moon cast an eerie light onto the Gulf, creating a silver glow on a large circle of waves. Damien opened the refrigerator, grabbed a cold soda, and walked over to the loveseat and joined Leslie. For the first time, he analyzed her physical shape and tried to mentally imagine what it would be like to sleep with her.

He looked at her lower body first, and worked his way up. Her thighs were the biggest parts on her body. When she walked, she had to sway slightly to keep them from scrubbing. Her waist was surprisingly small for someone her size. Her upper body was pretty normal, with the exception of some extra pounds that made her arms jiggle slightly when she reached out. Her breasts were small; a "B" cup, Damien presumed. He could work with that. Her face was her saving grace. Although she didn't look anywhere near as good as Cindy or Stacey in ANY department, she was cute. Her eyes had an oriental curve to them, her nose was slightly pudgy, and her lips were full. She had neck-length black hair that bounced with natural twists. The hint of bags under her eyes let Damien know that she lived a hard life up to this point. Maybe he could make her forget her worries for just one night.

After a few minutes of small talk, Damien made his move.

"Look Leslie," Damien said, while moving his left arm across the back of the loveseat behind Leslie's head. "I think you're pretty good looking myself."

"Yeah, right. Whatever you say, beer man." Leslie wasn't buying his head-bag-at-midnight booty call routine. She smelled the liquid barley on his breath.

"No, I'm for real. I'm not drunk either. I only had two glasses of beer. You really do look pretty good to me. I can prove it to you."

"How?"

Damien slid closer to Leslie, so close that she noticed the tent that had begun to rise in his pants.
"Whoa, Damien. You don't need to be that close up on me. I don't remember you wanting me so bad at Concepts. Seems to me you hardly speak, much less take an interest in how I look."

Leslie slid to her left, putting her hands out to curtail Damien's advances.

"C'mon, Leslie. Nobody has to know. We can go downstairs to the room and make love without anybody knowing about it."

Leslie could sense his desperation. She knew he was slightly drunk, so she tried to call it a night before the situation got out of hand.

"Look, I appreciate the affection, but I'm about to go to sleep… by myself." Leslie moved to get up, but Damien pulled her back down by the arm.

"C'mon Leslie, you know you want me." Damien tried to stick his tongue in her mouth, but he was unsuccessful. Leslie reared back and slapped the shit out of him.

"Smackk!!" The concussion her open left hand made on his right ear caused him to go deaf temporarily. A high-pitched tone drowned out any background ambiance. His hard-on immediately shrank to the size of a prune, and he could feel the clear semen beginning to stick to his underwear. He sat, embarrassed, while Leslie ran down the stairs, shocked and pissed off by what had just happened. She went into her bedroom, locked the door, and balled up under the covers. She didn't know whether to curse or cry, so she fell asleep instead. Damien sat for a few minutes recovering from Leslie's fatal blow, and then walked down the winding staircase to his room. He changed into his pajamas, went to the bathroom to brush his teeth, and lay down for the night with thoughts of sex rambling through his impatient mind.

* * *

8 Saturday Morning

Kelvin was jarred out of his sleep by the piercing sound of a digital alarm clock. He squinted his eyes a few times, adjusted his sight, and reached over to push the snooze button. The time read 7:15. After three more encounters with the intermittent buzzer, Kelvin finally mustered enough strength to roll himself out of the bed. He was a man of his word, and wanted to get an early start on breakfast, so Damien could enjoy the rewards of his winning bet.

After washing his face, shaving, and brushing his teeth, Kelvin threw on some blue jean shorts and a tan t-shirt that had the words "Underground Atlanta" stitched in blue on it. He slipped into some brown Jesus sandals, left the bedroom, and walked towards the kitchen to prepare breakfast.

"Good morning, Kelvin!"

The discernable voice caught him off guard. He looked to his right, and saw Stacey standing in the foyer holding what looked like a red two-piece bathing suit and a folded towel.

"Oh, good morning Stacey." Kelvin's voice was an octave lower than normal, and a bit raspy too. It was going to take a minute for his body to shake off the effects of his heavy snoring.

"What are you doing up so early?" Kelvin asked.

"I wanted to go down to the beach before everyone woke up and got going."

"Oh, okay. You hungry? I was just about to cook breakfast."

"No, not really. I might take a piece of toast though, just in case."

"One piece of toast, coming right up."

Stacey disappeared into the bathroom, and Kelvin went into the kitchen to make breakfast. He pulled eggs and bacon out of the refrigerator, grits out of the cabinet, a few bowls, and a pot and pan set out of the pantry. He retrieved some utensils out of a drawer, and went to work. He broke a dozen and a half eggs in a large bowl, seasoned them with a little Season-All, and filled a large pot with tap water. He turned one of the stove eyes to medium-high, and set the pot on it. As he prepared to make the toast, Stacey's voice broke the morning silence once again. Her head was peeking around the corner, and she made a request that caused Kelvin's heart to skip.

"Kelvin, could you help me out for a minute? I'm having technical difficulties." Her voice was low, so as not to wake anyone else, but loud enough for Kelvin to receive the message.

He saw enough of her to realize that she had the towel wrapped around her upper body. Her left hand was holding a red bikini top, and a "damsel in distress" look was etched into her face. Kelvin stopped what he was doing, put down the utensils, and anxiously walked around the corner to the bathroom. Before he peeked in, he asked Stacey if she was decent.

"Yes," she replied.

I wonder what she wants, Kelvin thought to himself. He was about to find out. Stacey's mom was known in Northwest Louisiana as the "Red River Flirt." As the Services Coordinator for the Shreveport-Bossier Convention Bureau, she enjoyed a string of job promotions due in part to her feline tactics when it came to corporate clients. First, she made certain that the city rolled out the red carpet for its prized guests and CEO's. Then, she wore provocative formalwear when escorting her male clients to dinner parties. By using subtle tactics such as kissing them on the cheek, rubbing their shoulders with her hands, or teasing them with a close dance, she was more than able to secure her share of contracts.

Stacey was an excellent observer, and enjoyed emulating her mom's business model. This morning, she wanted to practice on Kelvin, so she could parlay her flirting skills into a lead role on an R&B video shoot in the near future. She wasn't a home wrecker, but she certainly knew how to torture the male psyche.

"Come in," Stacey said softly. Kelvin's heart was beating so fast it felt like it was going to jump out of his chest.

"What's up?" Kelvin asked nervously, as Stacey stood in front of the mirror clutching the top of the towel with her left hand.

"I can't seem to get this bikini top latched up; do you mind helping me?"

Kelvin was stuck. Although he liked to flirt as well, he wasn't crazy enough to do it in the bathroom around the corner from his sleeping wife.

"O…okay," Kelvin responded. "I'll turn around while you get it started. Let me know when you're ready."

"Alright." Stacey dropped the towel with a sly grin on her face, and placed the bikini on her luscious, round breasts. "I'm ready."

Kelvin turned around, and reached his hands out to fasten her bikini's back closure. Suddenly, Stacey let go of her bikini top, revealing her well-endowed bosom.

"Oops," Stacey said, as she looked in the mirror to catch Kelvin's bewildered look.

Then, she bent over in front of Kelvin to pick up her top. Kelvin caught a glimpse of the rear of her stretch boy pant bikini bottoms; he was speechless. Sweating, he fastened the back of her bikini, and hurriedly vacated the tight confines of the bathroom. Stacey giggled quietly, wrapped her waist with a sheer sarong, and walked out the front door. *Funny*, she thought to herself. *Exposing a man to his vulnerability is like giving Superman a kryptonite ring for Christmas. He's definitely going to become weak.* She headed towards the back of the house, ascended the stairs to the deck walkway with her hair magazine and towel in tow, and walked towards the beach.

*   *   *

Leslie tossed and turned, as the smell of sweet bacon penetrated the downstairs rec room. She didn't sleep well at all, and the bags under her eyes looked like they were packed for a Hawaiian vacation. She sat up in her bed and absorbed the room's yellow décor. The multicolored bedspread was decorated with Seahorse prints over triangle shaped patterns. The blonde rug was low-pile and unstained, and identical framed prints hung on each wall next to the bed. Leslie sat and stared for what seemed like an eternity, not gazing at anything in particular, but thinking about everything imaginable.

In times like these, times when Leslie was hurt by a man, she wanted to give up, lie down, and die. It would be easier that way, she thought. Her parents always told her that if she kept searching, she would find "Mr. Right." So far, all she had ever found was "Mr. Wrong." Not that she wanted Damien by any means. In fact, he wasn't even her type. She didn't like pretty boys, she didn't like Kappas, and she definitely didn't like men under six feet tall. That wasn't her preferred profile. Leslie's problem was that men always treated her like a last minute piece of ass. That's what hurt more than anything else. Perhaps it was her attitude, she thought, that drove men away from her. Maybe they feared her blackness. Whatever the case, she was sick of playing third-string in the dating game.

As her thoughts focused on last night, she contemplated telling Felicia or Kym, and filing a formal complaint against Damien when she returned to Concepts. She didn't know what to do. But she knew one thing; she didn't feel like running this time.

She was tired of that. This time, she wanted revenge. Revenge for all of those miserable, lonesome nights. Revenge for suffering under Jimmie's warped theory of male domination. Revenge for being told she was too fat, too short, or too black. She was ready to exact justice on her tormentors, and unfortunately for Damien, he was the target.

Leslie stepped out of the bed with a newfound level of confidence. She gathered a change of clothes and a towel, and headed out towards the bathroom.

"Good morning," Antoine said.

"Good morning," Leslie responded. Antoine was sitting on the white chaise lounge that was situated against the outside wall of his room across from Leslie's. He was reading his Bible, trying to get some early morning inspiration.

"Doing some reading, huh?"

"That's part of my daily routine. Without Jesus, there would be no me."

"I heard that! Well, without a shower, the funk has the power!"

They both let out good, hearty laughs, and Leslie excused herself to the bathroom. Leslie's jovial demeanor surprised Antoine. Usually, she was a bit more reserved and melancholy. He tilted his head to the side, shrugged his shoulders, and got back to his Bible verse.

*   *   *

Kelvin had just pulled some Butter-Me-Nots out of the refrigerator when Felicia opened the door and walked into the living area.

"Good morning, baby. How long have you been up?" She reached into the air with her outstretched arms, and let out a massive morning yawn.

"Not too long," Kelvin said. "You hungry?"

"As a matter of fact, I am. Baby, I don't know what's gotten into you this weekend, but you sure are playing the part. It smells good in here. If you do this at home every morning, I might be calling in sick on a regular basis," Felicia said.

"Is that right," Kelvin replied. "Well, I tell you what. Find some mommy and daddy time in your busy schedule and you've got a bet."

Felicia walked up behind Kelvin and kissed him on the neck. She wrapped her arms around his body and squeezed his thick chest. They rocked gently from side-to-side, sharing a blissful moment. Kelvin turned to the side, grabbed Felicia's head, and kissed her on the lips. *These are the times that I crave,* Felicia thought. Kelvin was thinking the same thing.

"Do you mind knocking on Kym's door?" Kelvin asked Felicia.

"Isn't Stacey in there too?"

"No, she went walking on the beach."

"Oh, okay. I'll check on everybody downstairs, too."

"Thanks. I love you, sweetie."

"I love you too."

Felicia woke Kym up, and walked downstairs to get the others. She knocked on Damien's door several times before she got a response.

"Damien!"

"Yeah," he answered with a deep crackle in his voice.

"Kelvin is cooking breakfast. Come on and get up, so we can eat and take care of business."

"I'm coming." Damien rolled over and reached out towards the nightstand to pick up his chrome watch. It read 8:35.

Damien scratched his head a few times, breathed a few breaths of frustration, and pulled the covers back. Thoughts of Cindy were pasted onto his brain like colors on an abstract painting. All he could think about was getting with her tonight. He had been so busy at Concepts lately, he really hadn't had time to date. Besides a couple of average looking booty call girls, Damien had been on a dry streak. But that was going to have to wait until later. Right now, Damien was about to go upstairs to taunt Kelvin and enjoy his breakfast. He grabbed his white linen drawstring pants and a white v-neck tee out of his travel bag. He scooped his toothbrush off the nightstand, opened his bedroom door, and headed towards the bathroom.

"What's up Antoine," Damien said as he made a detour around the pool table.

"Good morning Damien."

"You coming up with some ideas for today?"

"No, just trying to remain blessed." Antoine peeled his hardback Bible cover back from its case and held it up slightly so Damien could see what he was reading.

"Oh, well assalamualaykum, my brother," Damien said, trying to be funny.

"Whatever," Antoine replied. "You need Jesus more than anybody in here. It's a wonder you haven't passed out trying to keep up with all your women. I don't see how you do it." Antoine shook his head slowly from side-to-side and looked back down into his Bible. Damien started walking towards the bathroom, but Antoine informed him that Leslie was finishing up her shower.

*   *   *

Kelvin didn't do too much cooking at home. He proved that yesterday on the grill. His shift schedule changed quite often, depending on production demands, leaving him either too tired or too late coming home to play "Chef Kelvin." However, when he got a chance to prove his culinary worth, he was more than willing to throw down in the kitchen. Kelvin turned the pot of grits down to the lowest setting, took the top off, and stirred with a long wooden spoon to get an even consistency. He cut half of a stick of butter, and stirred it into the pot. He opened the oven, pulled the bacon out, and replaced it with ten biscuits. He wanted this meal to be perfect, so he decided to use the bacon grease instead of butter to cook the eggs. He turned another eye on medium, waited a couple of minutes or so, and poured a third of the eggs into the skillet.

Using bacon grease to cook eggs is real country. That's something he learned from his mother Gloria. She made the best breakfast in the entire world, he thought, and he would die to have some right now. However, her diabetes made it impossible for her to eat unhealthy food. Three years ago, her doctor told her to lose weight and start eating healthy, or prepare her funeral arrangements. Seeing his mom eating fruits and salads and wearing a size twelve was weird for Kelvin. He was used to her looking like "Big Momma" from the plus size section. But if a change in her lifestyle was going to keep her around for a few more years, he was happy.

Kelvin scrambled the eggs well, just as Damien requested, and even melted some cheese on them. He cooked the next two batches of eggs, and poured them onto a large serving tray next to the bacon. He removed the biscuits from the oven, poured the grits into a metal bowl, and put four slices of bread into the toaster for Stacey and Damien. Kelvin was on a roll. He took a gallon of orange juice out of the refrigerator, and set the table.

"Breakfast is ready!" he yelled down the staircase, anticipating the satisfaction that everyone would get as they devoured his meal.

After exchanging a brief, intense stare with Leslie, Damien took her place in the bathroom. Leslie spoke to Felicia and went into her room to put up her belongings. Felicia was sitting next to Antoine on the chaise lounge talking to him about his interaction with Kelvin.

"Antoine," Felicia said. "You have to understand how Kelvin feels. He didn't even want to be here this weekend. I'm trying to make him feel comfortable, but he told me that you're making crazy comments towards him."

"What?" Antoine responded, putting his Bible to the side. "If anything, I'm the one who's the victim here. I was trying to make the brotha feel at home. He's the one who busted into our meeting yesterday with all of his bright ideas. He doesn't even work in our field. Then, he and Damien tried to clown me last night while I was trying to get some sleep."

"What did they do?" Felicia asked.

"They insulted me like I wasn't "One of the boys," as Kelvin put it, and then Damien made me flip a coin to see who would start their billiards game, like I was their servant or something. Then, your husband called me a table wimp and said I was one of the sorriest persons he ever played pool against. I started to cuss his ass out, but out of respect for you, I didn't."

"Okay Antoine, I apologize for Kelvin's antics, and I promise that I'll talk to him about insulting you, but you have a way of getting under people's skin too."

"Yeah? How so?" Antoine looked at Felicia with his eyebrows raised. He wanted an explanation.

"You have a way of alienating people who aren't up to your class standards."

Antoine shifted. "Oh, really."

"Yes. For example, we all know that if you cold-call a client who's on a tight budget, you will refer them to one of us."

"Yeah, but that's financial."

"Exactly, Antoine. And that attitude spills over into your personal life too. You look at people who are quote-unquote "beneath you" as far as their life's work or the size of their bank account, and you judge them without getting to know them."

"But I don't—" Felicia cut Antoine off in mid-sentence. She uncrossed her legs, turned towards him, and proceeded to read him like a dictionary.

"And then you try to embarrass me by belittling my husband in front of Stacey?"

"But Felicia, Kelvin was trying to—"

"No, Antoine. I know you, probably better than you know yourself. I am always there to listen to your problems. I know things that you haven't even told your fiancée."

"And visa-versa," Antoine quickly interjected.

"Yes, and I appreciate the ear, but what we share with each other needs to stay right where we put it; in each other's ear. Listen, Antoine. I don't want to argue with you. I just want to make my position clear. I am your co-worker. I am your friend. But first, I am Mrs. Sampson, wife of Kelvin, and mother of Jordan. And I will never let anyone or anything get in between that. If you want to be jealous, fine. But I want you two to stop acting like macho bullfighters and just relax. After today, neither you nor him will have to worry about entertaining each other. So please, do yourself and me a favor, and cease the insults, okay?"

"Yeah." Antoine got up, huffed a breath of air, and went to his room to put up his Bible. *So much for the morning inspiration,* he thought to himself. In a way though, Felicia was right. His grandparents had always talked to Antoine about values and friendship, but it seemed like the Atlanta lifestyle had gotten the best of him. In a city full of urban professionals, those who succeeded had double-dutched into the elite social circles and stayed there. Associating with those beneath you was faux pas and could result in an early career and social death.

It really started at FAMU, Antoine thought. Folks in the band were taught they were better than everyone, including the football players. They would always kid the athletes in the cafeteria about how they had practiced twice as long as them, and that people came to the games just to see the band. And although it was true, being in the most popular organization on campus seemed to have a negative effect on Antoine's personality. Even folks back home had noticed. Some of his neighborhood homeboys called him a sellout, and told him he wasn't welcome in the hood anymore. They said he didn't speak when he came home to check on his tenants, or come by to say hello to their families. *Seems ironic,* Antoine thought. *Folks tell you to do better, and when you do, they hate you for it.* He shook his head, laid his Bible on the dresser, and walked upstairs to join the others for breakfast.

"Good morning!" Stacey said, as she opened the sliding glass door. Felicia, Kelvin, Leslie, and Antoine were preparing their plates in the kitchen. Stacey bounced in like she was on top of the world, and she was. The morning air was refreshing to her, and the sight of all those birds flocking and singing and walking was amazing. She even saw fish shooting out of the water, as if to announce their arrival to the new day.

Felicia eyed Stacey up and down. *Her body is beautiful,* she thought. *I wish my body were in that kind of shape.* Leslie thought the same thing. Kelvin and Antoine just stared.

"Hi Stacey," Antoine said. Kym opened the bathroom door and walked around the corner. She had never seen Stacey's body either. Stacey usually dressed in business or business-casual wear at Concepts. Kym admired Stacey's physique and reminisced about when she played softball at Fullerton. *That was the last time I was in that kind of shape,* she thought. It was a lot of hard work, but it paid off in the end. Not only would you get compliments, she thought, but your self-confidence would receive a boost as well.

Kym spoke. "Good morning everybody, good morning Stacey. You look nice in that bathing suit."

"Thanks, Kym. It looks like breakfast is ready. I'm going to go change. You all go ahead and get started without me. Kelvin was thinking, *you don't have to change, that's just fine.* Stacey took the twelve-yard walk across the living area, and five pairs of eyeballs followed her every step. Her waistline was small, but her buttocks were shaped like twin basketballs. As she walked towards her room, it looked like a Harlem Globetrotter was performing a slow dribble on her backside.

Damien emerged from the stairwell just in time to catch Stacey's runway-like exit. His mouth dropped to his shoulder, and he grabbed the waist-high peach colored partition to keep from tumbling backwards. His face resembled Buckwheat or Alfalfa whenever they were shocked, and although it was embarrassing, his reaction was natural. Damien stood there looking dumbfounded, until Stacey's room door closed. Then, Felicia snapped him back into reality.

"Damien, snap out of it. Come and fix your plate."

Damien shook his head in disbelief, and walked over to the kitchen to join the others. Everyone took a seat, and Felicia led the prayer.

"Lord, as we prepare to break bread, let us remain humble and remember those who are less fortunate. Let us acknowledge our strengths, improve on our faults, and use this meal as fuel for prosperity. We ask that you guide us to the proper solution today, Oh Lord, and that you bless each and every person standing here with the strength to work through our differences. All these and others we ask in your son Jesus Christ's name, Amen."

Kelvin's head was down at the beginning her prayer, but he briefly looked up at Antoine. Antoine must have felt Kelvin's telepathy, because he looked up too. The two exchanged hostile glares, and looked back down until the conclusion of Felicia's prayer.

*   *   *

9   Saturday Morning

"Boy, Kelvin, you really threw down on this breakfast," Damien said.

"No problem, homeboy. Just make sure you get back at me on that pool table before we leave."

"I'm gonna to give you another chance today, but this time you're going to have to play with one hand tied behind your back."

Kelvin laughed, as he received compliments from everyone for cooking a slamming breakfast; everyone except Antoine.

Kelvin took all of the dishes up, and prepared to wash them. Felicia wanted to get an early start on the assignment, so they could enjoy all that the beach had to offer. She turned her wrist over to look at her brown Wal-Mart wristwatch. It read 9:42.

"Okay folks, Let's get down to business. Kym and I briefly reviewed all of your suggestions, and we saw some really good ideas in your notes. What we would like to do this morning is have you break off into groups of two, and share the ideas. After five minutes, you will rotate to someone else until everyone has heard your idea. Everyone should give each other critical feedback, and then we will revise our portions of the plan. After that, we will meet as a group to discuss the final proposal, which Kym and I will type after the meeting. Does that sound okay?"

Everyone nodded in agreement. Kym passed the notepads out to their respective owners, and powered on her laptop. She took the memory stick off of her key ring, and attached it to her USB port. Antoine did the same. Everyone worked in pairs, as Felicia timed their miniature information-swapping sessions. After a little over thirty minutes, it was time to come together as a group. Felicia prayed that everyone would remain professional and refrain from personal attacks. Kym was hoping the same thing. Even though she and Felicia were the official project managers, yesterday's encounter with Leslie left her feeling that she was not respected as one. She felt the best thing to do was to be a team player and lay low until they returned to Atlanta.

Damien started out. He presented his idea for the website design. Promoting networking mixers on the Internet in Charlotte and now in Atlanta lent him a higher level of expertise in this area.

"Okay," Damien started. "Basically, my idea is to revamp this website, inside-out. The front page is boring, the sitemap needs to be upgraded, menu-style, for easier access to the content, Shockwave graphics and music needs to be added to the presentation, maybe as a splash page, and the Atlanta Falcons need to be promoted on there in a major way. This website should be exciting. It should make people tell their friends and associates about it. All you have to do is check out Club Visions on a Friday night, and you will know that the proper website treatment will set your venue out. It doesn't hurt that they have the bomb facility, or invite popular music stars and entertainers to host their parties either."

"But do we want to alienate people trying to set up family reunions and business conferences?" Antoine asked. "Most of the business generated by the Convention and Visitor's Bureau comes from those sources. We definitely don't want to alienate them."

"Good point," Damien said. "And like I told you in our mini-group, we are going to have to find the right balance. That means they are going to have to find an outside design company who has developed similar sites that are tasteful. I checked out the Las Vegas CVB website, San Diego's website, and Miami's website. Each one offers something unique. If we blend together some of their ideas to incorporate on our site, we can't miss.

"That's a good idea," Felicia said. Kym, would you pull up some of those websites so we can see them?"

Kym obliged, and soon everyone was ogling over the websites of the various cities, especially Miami's. The models on the site were beautiful, and represented a variety of ethnic diversity. Everyone got the feeling that they were welcome to visit there, and got a taste of Miami's cultural flavor by exploring the site.

"Kelvin, come check this out," Damien said. Kelvin got up from the couch, and walked over to the table.

"If you didn't know anything about Miami, would you visit after looking at their Convention and Visitor's Bureau website?" Damien asked.

"Let me see," Kelvin said. Damien turned the laptop so Kelvin could get a better look.

"Hell yeah, I would visit. Look at those pretty girls. They're sipping on that wine too? If I was single, I'd be making reservations right now."

"See what I'm talking about?" Damien said. "It's all about the package. Nobody wants to see a picture of a fountain with little kids running through it. They want to see what kind of fun they can have AFTER they put the kids to bed."

Damien clicked the site map and went to the visitor's section. "See, they even have something for the ladies."

"Let me see that," Leslie said. Felicia stood up and peered over the shoulders of her gathered associates to see what Damien had to show them.

"Oh, my God," Leslie said. "Look at those bodies. Those men are too fine."

Felicia's face would have turned beet red if she was white, but she blushed the best that she could.

"But wait," Damien said. "The picture changes every time you leave and come back, watch."

"Daaiimm," Kelvin remarked. Felicia slapped him playfully on the back of his head. Damien rested his case.

"Okay," Felicia said. "Enough of the skin parade. Let's keep the momentum going." Felicia's leadership skills were being tested. The coup against Kym yesterday could have potentially undermined the entire project, but Felicia stepped in gracefully and handled the situation like a seasoned veteran. Without being specific, her vague message was received exactly the way she intended it to be. Everyone took his or her seats, including Kelvin. Kym closed the websites, and they prepared to get back to business.

Felicia continued directing the meeting. "Antoine, you're next. You worked on the marketing, right?"

"Yes, I did. Basically, I analyzed their existing marketing techniques, and tweaked them to improve on their effectiveness. Forrester Research published a survey of marketers a couple of years ago that included forty-seven managers. Basically, the results showed that many of their marketing techniques were out of date. For example, banner ads on the Internet were used by eighty-nine percent of the respondents, yet banner ads were ranked twelfth out of the thirteen most effective techniques of marketing.

"Well, what is the most effective technique then?" Damien asked.

"Affiliate programs and direct e-mail," Antoine said.

"Public relations should be high up there too," Kym said.

"It was," said Antoine. "As a matter of fact, it ranked third on the list. But I think they do a decent job of that now. The mayor's hands-on approach to guests, visitors, and dignitaries has a lot to do with that."

"So what is your final proposal?" Felicia asked.

"I would like to incorporate the most effective marketing techniques available, such as outdoor advertising, television campaigns, and e-mails. I would also like to improve on the ones they already have. The website is an excellent resource, but the delivery is flawed. If we strengthen their affiliate program and utilize some of Damien's suggestions, we should be okay."

"What about Kelvin's suggestions from yesterday?" Damien asked.

Antoine's face twisted with dismay, and he leaned over and planted his face between his hands. Kelvin had one ear on the TV, and one on their conversation.

"Look," Antoine said, "I personally have the same opinion as I did yesterday. I don't think that we should water the website down to appeal to the "hood." We are trying to attract businesses, families, folks who spend money."

Suddenly, twelve surprised eyes were focused on Antoine. Kelvin stood up from the wicker chair, causing it to squeak, and turned to face his nemesis.

"So what 'chu saying? You trying to say I'm from the hood?"

Felicia sensed the tension, as did everyone else. Normally, she would have played peacemaker, but this was her husband. Besides, she had already warned Antoine about making snide remarks in reference to her husband.

Antoine looked up from the table, turned his head to the side, and voiced his response.

"I'm not talking about you, Kelvin. All I'm saying is you need to do what you do, build cars or whatever, and let us handle our business."

Kelvin's face contorted with fury, like the possessed Good-Guy doll from the *Child's Play* movies. With tightly balled fists, he took a step forward in the direction of Antoine. Antoine could sense Kelvin's anger, and slid back from the table so he could utilize his peripheral vision, just in case Kelvin tried to steal him from the side.

"Nigga I'mma tell you like this; if you don't wanna hear what I gotta say, say it. But you come out of your mouth slick one more damn time, and I'mma bust your ass in the mouth."

Antoine made a motion to stand up and confront Kelvin, but Damien reached over and grabbed him by the arm. Antoine hadn't had a fight since his freshman year in college during an attempted hazing incident, but he was prepared. Being from Miami had taught him to learn a few things about survival. He wasn't small either. He stood just above six feet, and weighed a shade over 205. That made for an even match on paper. But Antoine had to remember that he was a new person now. He had to remember what his pastor preached about one Sunday. His sermon was titled, "How to Turn the Other Cheek."

"I'm alright," Antoine said to Damien, as he pulled his left triceps from his grip.

"Look Kelvin, I apologize for being rude, I was just trying to tell you that you should let us run this the way we've been trained to professionally, because we're the experts, that's all. I'm not going to say anything else about it either, because ultimately it's a group decision."

Kelvin didn't say a word; he just walked away in disgust, slamming the bedroom door behind him. Felicia glared at Antoine, a look that expressed her disappointment in him. He sat down, sighed a heavy breath, and tapped his pen nervously on the table as he waited for his heart rate to return to normal. Stacey was glad Kelvin cussed Antoine out. She always thought he was a bit arrogant. Leslie and Kym stared in disbelief at what had just transpired. The tension was once again thick, and needed to be sliced.

"You know what?" Felicia said, "Let's take a break. We'll reconvene in thirty minutes."

"Sounds good to me," Damien said.

"Me too," said Leslie.

Felicia went to the bedroom to check on Kelvin, and everyone else went their separate ways, except for Kym. She loaded up her instant messenger and checked to see if her friend was online. She saw that the code name was active, and clicked it so she could write a message.

MzKym: Hey U.
NvrtlU2b: how's it going?
MzKym: U won't believe!
NvrtlU2b: bad or good?
MzKym: Both, and crazy 2.
NvrtlU2b: oh boy. that sounds real interesting.
MzKym: I'll tell u more when I get back.
NvrtlU2b: okay, well try to enjoy the rest of your day, okay?
MzKym: Alright. HAK
NvrtlU2b: back to you.

Kym closed the instant messenger, and signed in to her e-mail service to check her messages. It was mostly Spam. Then, she went to a few search engines to research cruises to the Caribbean. *I can't wait to get back to Atlanta,* she thought to herself. *As soon as I get back, I'm taking a vacation to get away from all of this ignorance. I need to relax and unwind, get some ME time. Yeah, that's it... That's just what I need.*

*   *   *

After thirty-five minutes, Felicia opened the bedroom door. She had been talking to Kelvin, trying to calm him down and explain to him why Antoine was jealous. She didn't appreciate Kelvin showing out like that, but she understood why he did. She pleaded with him to keep quiet the rest of the day, and he reluctantly agreed. Felicia rounded everyone up, and the meeting reconvened.

"Where were we?" Felicia said.

"We were discussing the marketing strategy," Leslie said.

"Okay. Antoine, was there anything else you wanted to add?" Felicia said.

"Not really. I just want to apologize to everyone for causing a scene, and it won't happen again."

After a slight pause, Stacey's voice broke the mid-morning silence.

"Apology accepted," she said. "Yeah, apology accepted," echoed Damien. Slight head nods from everyone signaled that they were just ready to move on.

"Okay, Kym and Stacey, your turn. You two did the advertising, right?" Felicia said.

"Correct," Kym replied.

"We liked Antoine's proposal, so we focused on the television and outdoor campaigns. We found that a good commercial for the ACVB can be produced for less than one hundred thousand dollars, if we pull off some sponsorship. Also, we can run the ads in front of, or after prime time at a fraction of the cost. As far as the outdoor advertising, we researched the fourteen closest metropolitan cities to Atlanta from Lexington to Orlando. As far as rotary bulletins are concerned, the average price per city for a one year run was ten thousand dollars."

"What is a rotary bulletin?" Damien asked.

"A rotary bulletin is when your message basically moves around from one location to another at specific timeframes so the message can reach more people," Kym said.

"Oh, okay," Damien said.

Stacey chimed in with her information. "The permanent bulletins averaged seventy-two hundred dollars for one year, but the range was great. The cheapest we saw was twenty-four hundred, and the most expensive one was thirteen thousand."

"Okay, sounds good," Felicia said. She glanced at the brown clock on the wall above the television. It read 11:43.

"Okay, I want to be done by noon, so let's wrap this up. Leslie, you have the demographics?"

"I sure do, Felicia. Basically, I think the Bureau should retain their current clients, and just campaign more aggressively towards the younger demographic. Atlanta has lost some luster with the eighteen to thirty-two year old age group, especially since South Beach in Miami has gotten so popular, and the casinos in Mississippi have opened. We have Buckhead, but that scene has gotten stale. The traffic is bad, violence is common, and parking is way too high. We need some large events geared towards black college kids that are welcomed with open arms.

We also need to make business travelers aware of all the nice live jazz and spoken word events and venues around the city. It was a bad decision to stop Freaknik, because those kids were pumping millions of dollars into the economy. Those same folks are now going to the Biker Fest in Myrtle Beach, the beach party in Daytona, the Essence Festival in New Orleans, and whatever's going on in Miami. I think Kelvin's idea was excellent. If we piggyback off of the Falcon's success, it will be a win-win situation for everyone. We also need to include a plan for tapping into more minority conferences. We have nearly every ethnic group in the world living here, and need to focus on attracting their money here as well."

"That sounds good," Felicia said. "We can get to the specifics after our plan is approved, so we won't haggle over the details just yet. I looked at some preliminary figures for the cost of this plan, and it is going to be expensive. Television and outdoor advertising alone could cost upwards of half a million dollars. I set the bar at an even million for a six-month campaign that would start in August and run concurrently with the football season. If it is successful, we could extend it into next spring and summer."

"That sounds good," said Antoine. Kym agreed. "I think they will appreciate what we present to them as trying to maximize what Atlanta has to offer. Our city is on the verge of being considered a major tourist destination, and it has to be promoted as such. This might be the project that puts Concepts on the map."

"Let's hope so," Felicia said. "If there are no further concerns, then I consider this meeting adjourned. Pass your notes over to Kym and I, and we will type the proposal after lunch. Antoine has agreed to edit, right Antoine?"

"Sure, Felicia," Antoine said, with a reluctant smile. Felicia and Kym organized the notepads, and Antoine walked around the corner to the sitting room to check on Shauna. Leslie, Stacey, and Damien moved into the kitchen to make some sandwiches for everyone. Kelvin was knocked out in the master bedroom, taking a well-deserved nap. High noon was upon them.

*   *   *

10 Saturday Afternoon

"So what's up for this afternoon?" Damien said, as Leslie pulled the shaved deli-style turkey and ham out of the refrigerator. Stacey was unwrapping the cheese, and Damien was cutting thin slices of tomato and lettuce to go on the sandwiches.

"Nothing, that I know of," Stacey said. "I am probably going to go out and enjoy the beach again after I take a nap. I was up pretty early this morning."

Leslie was still perfecting her plan for revenge on Damien in her head, and she didn't want to let her anger foil the plot.

"Why don't you and Kelvin go to the store and get some drinks for later?" Leslie said. Her pleasant demeanor took Damien by surprise. Damien cut one last slice of tomato, placed the knife on the cutting board, wiped his hands on a paper towel, and turned around to face Leslie.

"What do you drink?" asked Damien, as he tried to peer into her soul and use his so-called mental telepathy to intercept Leslie's true thoughts.

"I'm not a heavy drinker, so coolers would be good for me," she replied nonchalantly.

Although her face exuded happiness, her eyes looked distant. Damien couldn't read her, couldn't tell where her head was after last night's misunderstanding. He wanted to apologize for what happened, but he didn't know how to approach her. To him, it was deja vu all over again. Just five months ago, a fellow co-worker had accused him of fondling her during his company's annual Christmas party in Charlotte. Damien thought it was a bunch of bullshit, because she had been flirting with him all night. It was cold as hell outside, and she walked in wearing a black fur coat, a sleek black sleeveless mini-dress, and four-inch heels. As she moved around the room, Damien could tell that she was hot. She walked up close to every man she approached, hugging and caressing his back as if she was begging for attention. When she finally made her way to him, he could tell that she had been drinking.

Lynda was usually reserved and very professional at work, but that night she was ready for some action. She damn near ran over Damien's date trying to get to him. She said she needed to discuss something with him in private, so Damien told her to meet him near the hallway bathroom in ten minutes. Damien excused himself from his female companion, who was boring him to death anyway, and made his way into the hallway. Lynda was already there, waiting like a possessed night cat, and she was looking FINE. She was accessorized from head to toe, wearing a sexy pair of platinum hoop earrings with bracelets to match. Damien even noticed the toe ring that she wore to bring attention to her perfectly shaped toes, which had a French pedicure. Her perfume caused every man in the room to take notice. It was sweet, sensual, and inviting.

Damien asked her what she wanted, and without saying a word, she pulled him by his jacket into the foyer of the women's bathroom and grabbed his crotch. She said something about wanting to make love to him and not wanting to be alone during the holidays while her husband was away on business. Although Damien was caught by surprise, he decided to take her up on the offer. He impatiently pushed her against the wall, grabbed her butt cheeks, and forced his tongue deep into her throat. As he

lap-danced in her mouth, his manhood began to swell, and he
started to grind against her crotch. He removed his right hand
from her behind and placed it on her left breast. Her C-cup was a
perfect fit, and he was about to remove it from her dress to suck
it when two laughing voices erupted out of nowhere. Damien's
startled eyes darted towards the left to see two of their co-
workers thoroughly enjoying the free peep show, as a sudden
rush of adrenaline surged through his heart. Lynda was so
embarrassed, she ran out of the foyer and straight to the elevator,
leaving her fur coat at the party. Realizing that Charlotte was
fairly small, Lynda knew it would only be a matter of time before
her husband, a big-time media executive, would be approached
by some little birdie about the party. So she did what any self-
respecting woman in her situation would do.

The following Monday, Damien was called into his
supervisor's office about an alleged sexual harassment charge
that was being filed by Lynda. Damien tried to explain the
situation, but it was useless. Sales at ICT had been down for
three consecutive quarters, and downsizing was the first and only
available option. Plus, word had gotten out that Damien was
using company time and computers to promote his networking
mixers. It was only a matter of time before Damien's relationship
with ICT would be terminated. Their only concession to him was
that they would highly recommend him to another employer,
which is how he ended up at Concepts.

"I want something stronger," Stacey said, with a serious look
on her face.

"Like what?" Damien said, turning his attention from Leslie.

"I don't care, I just want to get blitzed," Stacey said.

"Allriight girl!" Leslie said, expressing her empathy with
Stacey's emotional swell. The two slapped hands, and laughed as
if they were long, lost sisters who had just been reunited.

Stacey was tired of meeting, tired of pretending. Although
she was fairly new at Concepts, she was sick of playing the

"good girl" at work. *Tonight,* she thought to herself, *they will see the REAL Stacey.*

"What are you all talking about over there?" Felicia asked, as she and Kym finished organizing the notes.

"Oh, nothing Mrs. Samps... Oops, I meant nothing, Felicia." Stacey replied.

"That's better, Stacey. I hear an awful lot of giggling over there, you guys okay?" Felicia's den mother personality was at it again. Even though these were her co-workers, Felicia was the oldest, and somehow felt responsible for them while they were away from their natural environment.

"We're fine," Leslie said. "We're just laughing at Damien, that's all."

"Okay," Felicia said. "Is lunch ready?"

"Just about," Damien said.

"Just gotta make a few cups of ice, and we'll be ready for you."

"Sounds good," said Felicia.

*   *   *

Antoine sat down on the blue sofa, and dialed his house. No answer. He dialed again, this time from his phone book menu, just to be sure he had the right number. He rarely called his own house, because he was usually home, especially on weekends. On the third ring, Shauna picked up.

"H-Hello?" Shauna said. Her voice was barely audible, groggy and cracked, sounding like someone whose soul was beat down, trying to escape the energy of the world.

"Shauna?" Antoine said. "You sound like you're still knocked out. You must have had a late dinner last night."

"Yeah, it was kind of late when I got in. We got wrapped up in some church gossip, and the jazz band was fantastic."

"Well we've eaten breakfast, held a meeting, and are about to eat lunch. It's after twelve. You need to go ahead and get up. I left some cash in the vanity drawer for you to do some shopping for our trip to Miami. It is going to be real hot, and I don't want to be running around at the last minute like we did last time."

"Okay, I'm about to get up. I'll call you back when I get to the mall to see what you want to wear."

"Which mall are you going to?"

"Perimeter, and probably Lenox too."

"Okay. You sure that you're alright?" Antoine inquired. Something in the tone of Shauna's voice just didn't sound right.

"I'm okay," Shauna said.

"Okay baby, well I guess I'll let you go," Antoine said.

"Alright."

"I love you."

"I love you too."

Antoine pushed the red end button on his cellular phone, and stared silently at the blank television that sat in front of him. Something wasn't right. He could feel it. Maybe she felt guilty about moving in with him, he thought. He was the one that put pressure on her to make the decision, and he knew he would have to answer to her parents, but his deep-seeded feelings for her transcended rules, traditions, and even his religious beliefs. Shauna had blinded Antoine like a cavefish, and love was his prison.

As Antoine prepared to get up, he brushed his navy Versace cargo shorts with his hands and pulled his white Versace v-neck tee, trying to rid them of unwanted wrinkles. Antoine was obsessed with name brand clothing and personal hygiene. He took two, sometimes three baths a day, and even carried a pack of floss in his pocket at all times.

Being obsessed with perfection had become a full-time job for Antoine, a likely result of his broken childhood. Even though his adopted grandparents took care of him like he was God's gift to the world, the timing of their deaths and the revelation that came afterwards had a devastating effect on Antoine's psyche. He could not understand why they would keep such a terrible secret from him for so long. It would have been better, he thought, if they had told him about his family history while they were still alive. He was mentally equipped to handle the fact that his mom abandoned him, and his father was nowhere to be found. But having to deal with the fact that his grandparents kept such a secret, and waiting for the private investigator to confirm his family's past after they died was too much to bear.

* * *

Kelvin woke up to the sound of laughter and conversation. It was the first time all weekend that he didn't have any responsibilities. He lay in the queen-sized bed for a few more minutes, thinking about the conversation he had with Felicia about Antoine, and his promise to keep quiet.

There was something about Antoine that didn't sit right with Kelvin. Felicia admitted that she was good friends with Antoine at work, and promised him that nothing extra-marital was going on between them. Yet, Kelvin couldn't understand why someone who was just a friend would be jealous of his friend's husband, especially if he cared for her so much. Felicia explained that Antoine had been hurt in the past, and couldn't stand rejection. In their relationship, she was his confidant. So naturally, he would feel jealous if all of a sudden his comfort zone with Felicia was suddenly cut off by Kelvin's presence. Out of respect for Kelvin, Antoine had decided to distance himself from Felicia this weekend. He didn't want to impose on their personal space. However, he was not going to allow himself to be treated like a peon by Kelvin and Damien. The two men in Felicia's life had met at an impasse, and both refused to budge.

Kelvin finally sat up in the bed, and stared at his dark, naked torso in the mirror. He caressed his chest hairs, picking out the knots, and let out a wide yawn. He stood up, walked to the bathroom, and brushed his teeth. He grabbed a clean washcloth from the small linen closet, washed his face and essentials, and got dressed. After spraying his neck and the back of his hands with Burberry cologne, Kelvin brushed his hair, slid his sandals back on, and prepared to join the lunch crowd in the kitchen.

"So, what do you think Logan is going to say about this one?" Antoine said.

"I don't know," Felicia replied. "But I do know that this is a test for us. If our solution for this project doesn't fly, it will show that we can't work together on anything."

"True," Damien said.

Leslie felt uncomfortable participating in this "experiment." She even thought about filing a claim of workplace discrimination, but she didn't want to be blackballed. Nevertheless, she had a strong opinion, and needed to be heard.

"Why is it that they always have to pit us against each other? We always have to prove our worth, and usually it's at the expense of one of our brothers and sisters. I'll be honest. When you first approached us with this idea, I felt like we were being targeted. I still do, but what can you say when you have a mortgage, a car note, bills to pay, and groceries to buy?"

"I feel like it's an opportunity to prove we've got what it takes, and more," Stacey said. "If this plan works out, who knows, maybe we can form our own marketing company and make the money Concepts is making off of us."

"Sounds good," Felicia said. "But in the real world, we've got our own issues to deal with, and with no guaranteed income, I would be committing financial suicide."

"Right, plus some of us don't even get along," Damien said. Kym paid attention to her instincts and kept quiet. She wasn't about to get into it with Leslie again, even though she wanted to. Her schizophrenic, neo-political racism theories reminded her of Sistah Soljah, or Angela Davis. She wished that Leslie would just shut up sometimes and accept the fact that the world is the way it is, and that it wasn't going to change, not even for her.

"Well, at least we tried," Antoine said, as he leaned his elbows on the counter and took another bite out of his sandwich.

"We made a sincere effort at creating a viable plan for the bureau that reflects the entire culture of Atlanta, not just one particular aspect of it."

"I think we've done a good job; as a matter of fact, I'm going to claim that, in Jesus' name!" Felicia said, holding her right arm high in the air. Her hand waved back and forth, like she was riding at the head of a parade. Just then, Kelvin came out of the room looking refreshed. He spoke, took the sandwich and can of Coke that Felicia handed him, and headed towards the couch to watch previews of the NBA playoff game being played this evening. *If the Kings win tonight, the Timberwolves will be in trouble*, Kelvin thought to himself. He was a diehard Kings fan, and a lot of money was riding on the outcome of this series. He even allowed spreads in some bets with a few of his co-workers. Most of them were Timberwolves fans, especially with the recent MVP performances of Kevin Garnett. Kelvin wasn't concerned with the conversation in the kitchen. He was just ready to enjoy the game, get a good nights rest, and drive back to Atlanta. He was tired of trying to fit in. Ford was his home, and he was ready to get back.

Damien eased out of the kitchen and walked over towards the living area, where Kelvin had just sat down.

"Hey Kelvin," Damien said. Kelvin glanced up from the couch. He was expressionless.

"You wanna ride with me to the liquor store?"

"Yeah, I'll ride," Kelvin said, in a less than enthusiastic tone.

"I need to get some fresh air anyway."

"Alright, cool."

Damien walked back to the kitchen, grabbed the keys from off the counter top, and started back towards Kelvin.

"You going somewhere?" Felicia asked.

"Yeah, we're going to get something to drink for later on. You need anything?"

"No, I'm fine."

"I'll take a two-pack of BC powder," Leslie said.

"I'll take a pack of Kool Ultra 100's," Kym said. "Let me get my purse."

"Nah, I got it," Damien said.

"You sure?"

"Yeah, I'm straight. Anybody else?" Antoine and Stacey shook their heads no; Damien turned back towards Kelvin, and started walking towards the foyer.

"You ready?" Damien asked Kelvin.

"Yeah, let's ride." Kelvin wiped his hands on his napkin, took a long swig of his soda, and stood up.

"Be careful you two," Felicia said, in a concerned tone.

"Yeah," Kelvin responded, as if her motherly concern was getting on his nerves.

Kelvin and Damien stepped outside, squinted a few times, and allowed their eyes time to adjust to the brightness of the Florida sunshine.

"I'll drive, Damien," Kelvin said.

"You sure?"

"Yeah, man. I want you to check out my sound system. I've got some knock in my trunk. It ain't for sissies, so put something in your ears if you can't handle it."

"Man, you don't know who you're dealing with. I have a three thousand dollar system in my BMW," Damien replied. "I can skin a cat with my bass, probably move your house off its foundation. At the least, I'll damn sure wake up your neighbors."

Kelvin let out a hearty laugh, and they hopped in the Expedition to complete their mission. Best friends they weren't. But they had a lot in common. Kelvin was glad to find someone in corporate America that wasn't an asshole. Damien was a rider. Kelvin liked that.

*   *   *

Stacey and Leslie began cleaning the kitchen, as Kym, Felicia, and Antoine prepared to edit and type the proposal.

Felicia was ready to call Apreal to check on Jordan, but she was anxious to complete the proposal first, so she could relax. Leslie finally had Stacey by herself, and seized the opportunity to tell her about what Damien had done the night before.

"Stacey, I've got something to tell you," she said.

"Girl, what is it?" Stacey replied, as she ran the dishwater for the utensils and the cutting board. She looked at Leslie briefly, and saw a distressed look etched on her face.

"Last night, after Damien brought the pizza back, he tried to assault me."

"WHAT?" Stacey said in a low, firm tone. She shut the faucet off and turned towards Leslie. Leslie ran her hands nervously through her hair, and looked down at the floor momentarily. She gathered her composure, and moved next to Stacey so the others couldn't hear their conversation.

"He tried to rape me, Stacey," Leslie said.

Stacey was flabbergasted. She knew from her own experience with Damien that he could be aggressive, but she didn't know he was that belligerent.

"Girl, what happened?" Stacey said. She was all ears, and her eyes were as large as saucers. She placed her right hand on the kitchen countertop, and shifted her hips in anticipation of Leslie's account.

"Girl," Leslie said in a whispered tone, "He came back late, after all of you were asleep. We talked for a little while, he gave me a few compliments about how cute I was, which I knew was some bullshit, and the next thing you know, he's trying to come on to me."

"What did you do?" Stacey said, still shocked by Leslie's revelation.

"When I told him I was going to sleep, he pulled me back down on the loveseat and tried to stick his fucking tongue down my throat."

"Oh, shit!" said Stacey. "What happened then?"

"I slapped the living shit out of him."

"Daamn girl…"

"Then I ran downstairs, went into my room, and locked the door."

"Was he drunk?" Stacey asked.

"He sure smelled like it. He had beer all on his breath, and his speech was slurred."

"Why didn't you wake somebody up, girl? We would have whupped his ass."

"I was in shock, Stacey. I was scared; I didn't know what to do. If we would have been alone, there's no doubt in my mind he would have raped me."

"Damn girl, that is totally fucked up. What are you going to do about it? You going to file a police report, or what?"

"No, I'm probably going to report him to human relations when we get back. But before we leave, I've got a trick for his ass."

"What girl, because I want in. He tried me yesterday morning at the store," Stacey said. "He asked me if I have a man, like I owed him a response. Hell, I don't even know him like that. I started to read him the riot act, but Antoine saved his ass."

"Really?" Leslie said. "Well, I promise you one thing; after today, he'll think twice before he tries to stick his uninvited dick into the next chick. Let's finish cleaning the kitchen first, and then we'll get to work on that rat." Leslie and Stacey exchanged devilish grins, quickly cleaned up the remaining dishes, and wiped the counters. Leslie put the unused sodas back into the refrigerator, and closed the door. She glanced at the black stove, and read the green numbers on the digital clock. They read 1:38.

*   *   *

11 Saturday Afternoon

"Aaaaw, sookie now!" Damien was bouncing up and down, and side to side. Kelvin was old school, and liked R. Kelly because of his old school flavor. He was playing his Chocolate Factory CD, and R's smooth lyrics were crooning over a live flute and acoustic guitar.

Step, step, side to side, round and round, dip it now, separate, bring it back, (Now let me see you do the love slide)

Kelvin and Damien were in their groove, riding along with the windows down and the breeze blowing. As they approached the commercial area of the island, Kelvin turned the volume down on his sound system, to avoid getting a ticket. A sign posted at the island's entrance clearly stated that loud music would not be tolerated.

"There it is!" Damien exclaimed, as he pointed to the nondescript liquor store that sat on the right.

Kelvin slowed his approach, and wheeled his big-foot truck into the parking lot. He found an empty spot and pulled in. The sound of crackling gravel was pronounced, making it apparent that paved lots weren't a priority around these parts. The two got out, Kelvin set the alarm, and they approached the front door.

"What are we gettin'?" Kelvin asked.

"Leslie said she wanted some coolers, and Stacey said she wanted something hard," Damien said.

"Sheeeit, fine as she is, she don't have to go to the store to get that!" Kelvin exclaimed.

"I know that's right," Damien responded in agreement.

Kelvin entered the store first, setting off the jingling bells. Damien followed, feeling instant relief when a gust of cool air brushed across his perspiring face. They looked around, and began perusing the isles in search of some firewater for the night. The clerk, an older white man sporting a salt and pepper beard and a multicolored Hawaiian shirt pushed his glasses down and spoke to them in a thick Southern accent.

"You fellas need some help?"

"Yeah," Kelvin said. "What kind of coolers do the ladies like?"

"Oh, they like all kinds. But the ones that sell the most are Bacardi, in all flavors."

"Is that straight for you?" Kelvin asked, as he turned towards Damien.

"Yeah, I'm not picky."

"Okay, thanks," Kelvin said to the clerk.

"No problem. There are some cold ones in the back cooler over there."

The pair made their way towards the back and grabbed two six-packs of Pina Colada and Strawberry Daiquiri wine coolers out of the cooler.

"What do you drink, bruh?" Damien asked Kelvin.

"I'm from the old school," Kelvin said. "I drink Cognac; you know, Hennessy, Courvoisier, the good stuff. How 'bout you?"

"I drink whatever; beer, margaritas, martinis, anything with some flavor," Damien said.

"Let's go with the martinis then," Kelvin said. "The ladies at the plant go to happy hour on Fridays, and all they talk about is Appletini this, and Appletini that."

"That sounds like a winner. Let's do it," Damien said.

They perused the isles until they found all of the drinking ingredients and some plastic martini glasses; Kelvin grabbed a fifth of Hennessy, just in case. They looked like candidates for Alcoholics Anonymous, with the wine coolers tucked securely under their arms, and the liquor bottles in their hands. Damien had to juggle the Sour Apple Pucker so it wouldn't slip from his medium-sized fingers. Kelvin probably could have carried everything. He looked experienced doing this, and his hands were big, almost twice as thick as Damien's, and at least half an inch longer. They took everything to the counter, asked the clerk for some BC powder and a pack of Kool Ultra 100's, paid for their order, and headed out into the parking lot towards Kelvin's metallic green urban monster truck.

"Look man," Kelvin said to Damien as he placed the brown paper bag on the floor behind the driver's seat. "I'm not trying to show out on your co-worker, but it seems like he's had an attitude towards me ever since we got here. What's up with him? Does he act like that all the time?" Kelvin glanced over at Damien with a serious look, closed the rear passenger door, and climbed into the driver's seat.

"You know what," Damien said, as he closed the rear passenger door on his side and opened the front passenger door to get in. "I don't really know Antoine all that well, but in the few times I've been around him, I must say that he has had an attitude like he's better than me or something. I think he's jealous, because he knows I pull all the honeys, while he has to go home to the same woman every night."

"I hear you," Kelvin said, as he put the Expedition in reverse.

"Look man, I'm not trying to get you involved in my personal business, but when you're at work, is he around Felicia a lot?"

Damien turned towards Kelvin, wondering where he was going with his inquiry.

"Nah, not really; I mean, not more than a co-worker has to be around his associates. Most of us work on our own projects, so we're doing our own thing most of the time."

"So they don't hang out at work more than anybody else?"

"No, I wouldn't say that. They do eat lunch together from time to time, but that's about it."

"Alright, we'll I'mma tell you. I don't like his vibe. Any man that can talk to my wife should be able to talk to me, know what I'm sayin?"

"Yeah, I feel you," Damien said. He didn't like getting into other people's business, especially married people. He quickly changed the topic of conversation, so as to avoid becoming a participant in the triangular drama that was building between the three.

"You ever been here before?" he asked Kelvin, as they rode silently down the road towards the beach house.

"Naw, man. This is my first time going to the beach, period." Kelvin's face looked dejected, as if an arrow had been thrust through his heart.

"What!" Damien exclaimed. "You've never been to the beach in your entire life?"

"No. That's something I missed out on. My momma was too busy raising three boys and trying to keep bread on the table to take us anywhere, so we just got used to it. The only water I've seen is a couple of pay lakes that me and my Uncle Jake used to go to."

"You never wanted to take Felicia and your son to the beach?"

"Not really; not until I saw this place. Felicia went to the Bahamas with some of her girlfriends from church a few years ago, and she talked about how pretty it was. I even saw the pictures, but I wasn't paying it no attention. Now, I regret not going sooner. But I made a vow to myself yesterday that I'm gonna change. I'm going to take my son places I've never been, expose him to stuff my sorry-ass daddy wasn't around to expose me to. All he did was try to kick our asses when he got drunk. But when we got older and bigger, we put something on him that he'll never forget."

"Damn, bruh. I'm sorry to hear that. Well, the least you can do is enjoy the rest of this weekend. You're here now. Don't worry about Antoine. Believe me, the way Felicia talks about you at work, you're THE man."

"Thanks man," Kelvin said, as they slowed to make a left at Paradise Lane.

*   *   *

"We're going downstairs for a little bit," Leslie said to Felicia, Kym and Antoine, as she and Stacey started their quick descent down the half-winding stairwell. Stacey was anxious to see what Leslie had up her sleeve. *Leslie is sure playing it cool,* she thought. *If that was me, Damien would be locked up in that raggedy-ass looking trailer they call a sheriff's office, all alone with Barney Fife and the boys.*

Once they reached the bottom, Leslie motioned for Stacey to sit down at one of the mini-bar stools. She looked around nervously, as if she was checking to see if someone was coming down the stairs. She paused momentarily, and then reached down and pulled a small, crumpled piece of paper from her front pocket. She held it in her hand, and pulled out the stool next to Stacey. Stacey stared impatiently as Leslie got herself situated. Finally, she was ready to reveal her plan for revenge.

"Stacey," Leslie said. "My parents were Black Panthers. I could go running to the police, but that goes against what I was taught growing up. That would be my last resort. I like to handle

my own business. I'm going to take this nigga to the next level."
Her hand still clutched the paper, as if she held the winning Big
Game ticket on a fifty million dollar jackpot.

"C'mon girl, show it to me," Stacey said, as she shifted in
the brown pleather stool. Leslie uncurled her fingers, lifted her
right arm, and deposited the piece of paper onto the mini-bar's
medium-brown countertop. Stacey quickly unfolded it, and saw a
name, along with ten digits.

"Cindy? Who is Cindy?" Stacey asked Leslie in puzzlement.

"I don't know," Leslie replied. "But it seems as if our little
friend has met another victim since we got here. Look at the area
code. 850 is the local area code."

"Hmmm," Stacey mumbled to herself. "The name sounds
white, too."

"Yep. And I guarantee he's trying to line that up for tonight.
That's why it took so long for him to bring that pizza back last
night," Leslie said.

"Damn, girl, where did you get this from?" Stacey asked, as
she slid the piece of paper back towards Leslie.

"He left it on the bathroom countertop. A player always has
a plan "B." My brother taught me that. Problem is, Damien got
caught slipping."

"So what are you planning to do with that?" Stacey said.

"I'm going to call her."

"And mess his game up?"

"Not quite. If I play this right, she'll be on our side."

"Okay…" Stacey responded, unsure of what Leslie had
planned.

"C'mon, girl. Let me show you some game from the Chi."

Leslie pushed her stool back, grabbed the number, and
headed towards her room. Stacey quickly followed, trying to
anticipate her next move. Leslie closed the door behind Stacey,
locking it just in case Felicia or Antoine came looking for them.
She sat on the edge of the bed, grabbed the phone off the

receiver, and dialed. After three rings, a female answered the phone.

"Hellew?" The valley-girl slang immediately confirmed Leslie's deductive reasoning. She was white.

"Is this Cindy?"

"Newh it's nooot, would you like to speak with her?" It was Brooke.

"Yes, please," Leslie responded, already annoyed with the smart-alecky voice on the other end of the phone.

"Hello?" This time, the voice was mildly pleasant, even reserved.

"Cindy? Hi, I'm Leslie. I'm one of Damien's co-workers."

Stacey was all ears. This took her back to her high-school days, when she and her friends would test the honesty of the new guys they met by having their friends try to seduce them. If they were dumb or stupid enough to fall for it, they would call him on three-way, and listen to the Negro beg for hours, telling them that no one would know, and that he could keep a secret, and any other lame excuse he could come up with. They only wished they could see the look on his face when the friend started cussing him out for being a stupid dog, and that now he wouldn't be receiving sex from either one of them.

Stacey moved closer to Leslie's ear, stretching her body across the length of the bed. Leslie leaned over, close enough for Stacey to spy on their conversation.

"Damien?" Cindy tried to play dumb, but Leslie checked her in her tracks.

"Yeah, the guy you met yesterday. You did give somebody your number, didn't you?"

"Oh, okay. Come to think of it, I..."

"Never mind that," Leslie said, cutting Cindy's response short.

"We're not lovers or anything, I just called to warn you about him."

"Really?" Cindy said. She sat up from her beach chair, and planted her feet in the warm, white sand. She was all ears.

"Yes. Damien doesn't care about you. He's just trying to have sex with someone before he leaves this island."

"He told you that?"

"No. He already tried. He proposed to my other co-worker, and then he tried to force himself on me last night when he came back with some pizza."

Cindy was in shock. Damien seemed like such a nice guy to her. He was very courteous to her and her friends at the store and at the pizza parlor. She didn't know whether Leslie was joking or not, so she continued to talk.

"Have you been co-workers for long?"

"Damien has only been with our company for three months, so we don't know him like that," Leslie said. "Did you have plans with him for tonight?"

"We were talking about it, but nothing was solid," Cindy said.

"Well, if I were you, I would play it safe. You don't know what'll happen if he gets you alone, and I don't want to read about you in the newspaper. But I tell you what. I have a little plan that will teach Damien a lesson about respecting a woman's private property, and I'm going to need your help."

"Will I be safe?" Cindy asked, as she nervously ran her fingers through her hair.

"Yes. You will be coming over to our place. There are two other men here, and four women. We'll make sure that he doesn't go too far with you. We've got you covered."

"Okay, well what's the plan?

Leslie and Cindy hashed out their hit on Damien, while Stacey listened in awe. *Leslie is cunning as hell,* she thought to herself. *She's going to beat the boy at his own game. He doesn't know what he's got coming.* Stacey heard the loud voices of Kelvin and Damien as they walked in upstairs. They were kicking it like homeboys from back in the day. She tapped Leslie on the shoulder, and whispered for her to get off the phone. Leslie and Cindy said their goodbyes, and hung up. Stacey walked out of the room, and played lookout for Leslie. She stood to the side of the stairwell, just out of view in case one of them walked down. She gave Leslie the signal, and Leslie crept silently to the bathroom to place the piece of paper back where she had found it. She wanted this to be perfect. It was only right.

*   *   *

12 Saturday Afternoon

"Hey baby," Felicia said, as Damien and Kelvin rounded the corner from the foyer entrance.

"Hey," Kelvin responded, eyeing Felicia and Kym. Antoine didn't speak, nor look up. He continued creating charts and graphs on his Excel program for the proposal, as if Kelvin and Damien weren't there. Damien spoke, and they headed towards the kitchen to deposit their liquor stash in one of the cabinets.

"What's up with some more pool?" Damien asked Kelvin, as they took the bottles and six-packs out of the brown paper bags.

"You tell me," Kelvin responded sarcastically. "Seems like you're the one who flaked out on me last night. I know what's up though. You're scared I'll wipe your wallet out, so I won't even charge you today."

"Nah bruh, it ain't even like that. I just don't want any hard feelings, that's all. Tell you what. Let's play for beer shots. That way, it's a win-win situation."

"Sounds like a winner," Kelvin said, as he leaned down to put the coolers into the refrigerator. He closed the door, wiped his hands with a paper towel, and headed towards the stairwell.

"C'mon, Damien, let's roll."

Damien popped up from the counter he was leaning on, and followed in stride. As they started their descent, Antoine snuck a suspicious glare at Kelvin. Kelvin did the same, and turned his attention towards the stairwell.

"Ummph." The sound Kelvin elicited alerted Damien that something interesting awaited his eyesight. He took the last two steps, and stared to his right. Leslie and Stacey were outside on the deck leaning on the rail, facing the Gulf. They noticed Kelvin and Damien, but turned and continued their conversation as the tropical view serenaded their senses.

"Woo-ooh, what a stallion," Damien remarked, as he caught Stacey's backside with his eyes. "I didn't know she was THAT fine." The thin material on her white French Terry Capri pants accented every curve perfectly. Her matching tube top exposed the crest of her bosom, and a flash of silky, bronze skin peeked out near the top of her waist. It was much different from the business casual attire that she usually wore at Concepts. They could barely keep their eyes off of her, as they replenished the ice in the cooler, and re-stocked it with the last few beers.

"Man, I ain't even looking at that no more," Kelvin said. "It might cause me to lose."

Damien agreed. "Alright, let's play."

They rubbed the heads of their sticks with chalk, and got their pool game underway.

*　　*　　*

"Okay, looks like I've got the visuals in some kind of order," Antoine said. "Where are you guys?"

"We're on the last few lines," Felicia said.

"Thank God," Kym chimed in. "This has been interesting, to say the least."

"I know, girl," Felicia said. "Well, at least we have something to show Logan when we get back. I was beginning to think we wouldn't make it to this point."

"Amen," Antoine said from across the table.

"Kym, do you mind wrapping this up for me? I need to check on my baby. I didn't talk to him last night, and it's been nagging me all morning."

"No, no, you go ahead and call Jordan. I've got this. Antoine, will you look over this and proof it for us?" Kym said.

"Yeah, I got you. Go ahead, Felicia, we're cool."

"Thanks, guys." Felicia pushed her chair back, took a well-deserved stretch, and walked down the hallway towards the master bedroom.

Antoine seized the opportunity to apologize to Kym on behalf of affluent and culturally sensitive African-Americans across the United States.

"Kym, what happened yesterday was unfortunate, and I would like to apologize on Leslie's behalf. I think we were just as shocked by Leslie's comments as you were, and that's why no one jumped in sooner. Personally, I was appalled by her behavior, and I want you to know that what she said was not representative of the entire group. As a matter of fact, I have friends from across the entire rainbow. As a Christian, I don't feel anyone should be berated because of his or her culture or ethnic background. We all have to work together, regardless of where we came from."

"Thanks, Antoine, I appreciate that. We spoke yesterday while you were asleep, so I'd rather not go into it again."

"Okay, but if you need to talk, I'm always available."

"Thanks." Kym flashed a half-smile, and focused her eyes back onto her laptop. She wasn't in the mood to be lathered by Antoine's apologetic brownnosing. In her mind, she had a clear vision of all those eyeballs staring at her when Leslie asked about her college application, Antoine's included.

"Apreal?"

"Hey girl, how's the beach?"

"It's fine. We just finished our proposal, so I can finally get some rest." Felicia could hear the chorus of boys screaming in the background.

"Girrl, it sounds like you've got your hands full. What are the boys doing?"

"Child, I set up activities for them in the family room. They've got Nerf basketball, Playstation, Beyblade, and some kind of contraption that Jeff brought him for Christmas that launches racecars up a ramp off into the air. I've got our neighbor Durant, and his brother too. I told their momma to go enjoy her shopping. Next week, it'll be MY turn to hit Stonecrest."

"Whew! Girl, I feel for you. You definitely deserve a break. When I get back, we need to let our husbands enjoy some quality time with their sons, while we treat ourselves to some shopping and a day spa treatment."

"Sounds like a date. Anyway, I know you called to speak to that big-head boy of yours, so hold on." Felicia let out a laugh, while Apreal tried to ply Jordan apart from the human entanglement that had formed on the family room floor. The boys were tickling each other while simultaneously trying to wrestle the Nerf basketball from the scrum. They were definitely having a wonderful time.

"Hello?" Jordan's juvenile voice cried over the phone.

"Hey baby!" Felicia yelled out. From her excitement, you would think they had been separated after his birth.

"Hi, mommy!" Jordan responded, sounding just as excited.

"Are you having fun?"

"Yes."

"Are you being good?"

"Yes."

"What are you doing?"

"Playing."

"Are you ready for mommy to come back home?"

"No."

"You're not?"

"No. Where's daddy?"

"He's downstairs with his friend."

"Can I talk to him?"

"I'll tell him to call you later, okay?"

"Aww… I gotta go mommy, okay?"

"Okay, baby. Give me a kiss." They shared a phone smack, and Jordan was out. Apreal got back on the phone to say goodbye to Felicia.

"Girl, does it sound like he's in good hands?"

"Yes, girl. It sounds like he doesn't want to leave." The two shared a few more laughs, and hung up the phone. Felicia went into the bathroom, brushed her teeth, washed her hands and face, in preparation for an afternoon nap. She slipped out of her clothes, put on one of Kelvin's long t-shirts, pulled the comforter back, and crawled underneath the sheets. The sound of the rotating ceiling fan quickly lulled Felicia into a deep slumber.

*   *   *

Antoine was in the middle of proofing the proposal when his cell phone rang.

"Hello?"

"Hey, I'm at the mall." Shauna was awake now. Her late night session with Trevor had sapped her body emotionally and physically. She now sounded close to her normal self.

"Okay, which one?" Antoine asked.

"Lenox."

"Ahh, good choice. I knew my baby had taste. I saw some good-looking chino shorts in a Banana Republic ad last week. Could you pick those up for me, and a polo shirt too?"

"Sure, honey. Any particular color?"

"No, just make sure it's light. It's supposed to be hot down in Miami, so I want to be comfortable."

"Okay; how much can I spend?" Shauna always asked this question out of courtesy. As usual, his answer was predictable.

"As much as you need. I want my baby to look nice, and there's no price on that."

"Okay, I'll be good."

"Shauna?" The phone signal started to fade. Antoine stood up and walked towards the foyer to avoid the static.

"Shauna?"

"Yes?"

"I lost you for a minute… bad signal. Look, if you're feeling uneasy about our living situation, I do understand. I was going to call your parents and tell them what was going on, but I think I'll wait until I get back so we can think about this. If you change your mind, we still have time. You haven't sold your place yet."

"Okay, sweetheart. But let's talk about this some other time. I just want to enjoy myself right now, with no worries and no stress. Adrienne is supposed to meet me in the food court in a minute for lunch."

"Okay, I don't want to mess up your girls day out. You all have fun. Tell Adrienne I said hello. I love you."

"Love you too."

"Bye."

"Bye."

Shauna's eyes rolled back in her head as she hung up the phone; she let out a deep sigh of frustration. Between ending her relationship with Trevor, and her suffocating engagement with Antoine, Shauna felt like disappearing into a foxhole. She just hoped that she was making the right choice by getting married. It's not that she didn't love Antoine; she basked in his affection, loved the way he worshipped her, but she was beginning to miss her independence. And it seemed like the closer it got to their wedding date, the more possessive Antoine was becoming. In a way, Antoine seemed paranoid. And to Shauna, that was eerie; but to back out now would be disappointing to her friends, family, fellow church members, and most of all Antoine. He would be devastated. And that would rest on her conscience forever.

Kym turned the corner just as Antoine exited the sitting room. She could tell by the look on his face that something was bothering him.

"Antoine? Are you okay?" she asked.

"I'm alright," he said as he fumbled with the waist clip for his cell phone.

"Something you want to talk about that doesn't concern me?"

"It'll work itself out, I'm trusting in the Lord that it will."

"Look, why don't you join me outside. I'm going to smoke my cigarette. The least I can do is keep you company."

"Thank you, Kym. I really appreciate that." Antoine took her up on the offer, and they went outside on the front porch to doctor on each other's emotions.

*   *   *

"Blaww!" Damien added special effects to his winning shot, as he leaned across the table. The black eight ball sped quickly to the right corner pocket.

"Yes! Drink up my brotha!" Damien reveled in his victory, anxious to see Kelvin gulp down eight shots of beer.

"Awww man, you KNOW that was luck," Kelvin shot back, as a look of frustration settled across his sweating brow. Even with the air condition blowing full blast, it felt like a steam bath downstairs, due to the thick humidity that lingered outside and the Florida sunshine that poured through the glass panels.

The truth is, Kelvin never played hard without money on the table. Plus, he admired Damien's gusto, and didn't want to bruise his ego. Kelvin was pretty good at reading personalities, and from what he could tell so far, Damien's had a rough edge to it. Corporate America meets the streets. White collars and ties versus linen outfits and gator shoes. What a combination. *As long as he's happy,* Kelvin thought, *so am I.* Kelvin slapped hands with his new playing partna, gave him a friendly pat on the back, and pursued his punishment.

"So I guess it's eight to the head, huh?" Kelvin said, as he put his cue stick up.

"You know it," Damien responded. "However, if you want to make it interesting, we can flip a quarter... If I win, you have to add three more beer shots. If you win, I have to take three of yours. Fair enough?"

Kelvin laughed heartily. "Sure, let's do it." As Damien fumbled in his pocket for loose change, Stacey opened the sliding glass door; she and Leslie had just returned from a short walk on the beach.

"Hey, ladies," Kelvin said, as they entered the house.

"Hello," they responded, sounding jovial and pleasant. Damien still didn't trust Leslie's behavior after last night; to him, it was almost as if she had forgotten what happened.

"Could one of you flip this coin for us?" Damien asked.

"Sure!" Leslie said. Damien handed her the quarter nervously, being careful to avoid eye contact.

"Oh, here's your BC powder Leslie," Kelvin said, as he reached into his left front pocket.

"Ooh, thank you Kelvin, that was right on time," Leslie said. Stacey stood with her arms folded, waiting for Leslie. She was observing Damien's movements, analyzing his gestures, trying to pick up any sense of guilt. She noticed that he avoided eye contact with Leslie, a sure sign that something probably had gone wrong in the wee hours of the early morning.

"C'mon, girl, flip that thang!" Kelvin said, playfully scolding Leslie.

"Alright, alright." She walked over to the pool table, fixed the quarter between her thumb and her index finger, and let it fly.

"Heads!" Damien called, as it rotated through the air.

"Yeah, fool!" Kelvin yelled out, as the coin rested on tails. Leslie and Stacey excused themselves, as Kelvin and Damien proceeded to slurp down their cold shots of beer.

*   *   *

13 Saturday Evening

Felicia's eyes jolted open, as the shock of her nightmare caused her heart to race violently. She was dreaming that Apreal called her cell phone, screaming "Felicia, Felicia, oh my God!" frantically at the top of her lungs. Her motherly instincts immediately signaled that it was Jordan. As soon as Apreal began to tell Felicia that he was missing, she woke up. Felicia quickly slid out of the bed, grabbed her purse off of the dresser, and fumbled through it to retrieve her cell phone.

No missed calls. Whew! Felicia thought to herself. She started to call Apreal again, but knew she might get read the riot act. Instead, she gathered her composure, and went into the bathroom to brush her teeth. Her stomach was beginning to growl, and the sun was headed towards the horizon. She changed into some blue jeans and a white, short sleeve Henley that Kelvin brought her for the trip, combed her hair out, and headed out to see what everyone wanted to eat for dinner.

"Hey guys," Felicia said, as she approached Kelvin and Damien in the living area. They had come upstairs to watch the basketball game and let the cold beer settle in their stomachs.

"Hey Felicia," said Damien.

"What's up, sleepyhead," Kelvin echoed.

Felicia leaned down, gave Kelvin a peck on the cheek, wrapped her arms around his shoulders, and squeezed tight.

"Aww, look at the lovebirds," Damien said playfully, as he chuckled at their embrace.

"That's right," Felicia said. "One day this will be you."

"Oh, I don't know about that," Damien said. "The women in my life are like psychiatric patients; they all have different needs. And at that rate, I'll never be able to have just one."

"That's a bad excuse for being a dog, Damien," Felicia said. "Sooner or later, it's going to catch up with you, right baby?" Felicia looked down at Kelvin, whose eyes were locked on the playoff pre-game show.

"Uh, huh," Kelvin said, shaking his head like he was paying attention. Damien looked at Kelvin, and then Felicia, and let out a sarcastic laugh. Felicia slapped Kelvin lightly on the head, and headed towards the table to clear off the paperwork from the marketing project.

"Where is everybody?" Felicia wondered out loud.

"Leslie and Stacey said they were going to ride around the island for a little while; Kym and Antoine were on the front porch, but I think they took a walk down the road," Damien answered.

"What do you all want to eat tonight?" Felicia said. "I looked in the yellow pages yesterday, but I didn't see too many carry-out restaurants on the island. Most were across the bridge on the mainland, which is about a forty-five minute ride, round trip. They do have some good dine-in restaurants, though."

"I'm not going anywhere," Kelvin said. "I'll be right here, watching the game."

"What time does it start?" Felicia asked.

"Six o'clock," Kelvin said. Felicia glanced at the wall clock. It read 5:48.

"Alright then, how about some pizza?"

"Cool," Kelvin answered. Damien's face frowned up, because he had enough pizza the night before to last a week, but he wasn't about to complain.

"Damien, is that alright with you?" Felicia asked.

"That's fine. I don't have a preference."

Felicia finally left the guys alone, so they could enjoy the game. She went back to the room, opened the yellow pages, and placed an order for several pizzas. She was told they would arrive in about an hour. She hung up the phone, unzipped a medium-sized duffel bag that she had packed with board games, and looked for one to play after they ate. *Taboo? Nahh*, she thought to herself. *I don't want Kelvin to feel embarrassed again. Trivial Pursuit? Nah, that might be too boring.* She finally settled on the timeless classic board game, Monopoly. She put the other games back, zipped the bag up, and headed back to the living area to prepare for the evening's festivities.

*   *   *

"Boo yaw!" Kelvin yelled excitedly, as one of the Kings players drilled a three-point shot from beyond the white arc. "I told you, I told you! They don't want none of this! They're scared! What up, folk!" Kelvin leaned over and pushed Damien's leg. Damien had a dejected look on his face. Although he wasn't a huge sports fan, he admired the Timberwolves for their hunger and energy.

"It's only the end of the first quarter, B," Damien responded. "The T-wolves will come back; they always come back."

"I hear you, man. Time will tell." Kelvin reached for the glass of water Felicia brought him. She had smelled the pungent odor of beer on his breath, and didn't want him to get too carried away. Damien excused himself during the commercial break, and jogged downstairs to his room. It was after six-thirty. It was time to set up his date with Cindy for tonight. He opened the nightstand drawer to retrieve Cindy's telephone number. *Damn,* He thought to himself. *What did I do with her number?* He put his brain in reverse, trying to mentally re-create his movements for the day, and through the process of elimination, realized that the last place he remembered having her number was in the bathroom this morning. He walked swiftly out of his room, around the pool table, and into the bathroom. Luckily, it was in the exact spot where he left it. He took the crumpled piece of paper, unfolded it, and walked back to the room, relieved that he had found it. He sat down on the edge of the bed, pulled out his calling card, and dialed her digits.

"Hello?" Cindy's voice sounded good to Damien. It was soft, alluring, and innocent. Damien had only been with one white girl prior to meeting Cindy, but she acted dingy. Cindy, however, was cool as water. He knew he had to play this one right.

"Hi, Cindy, this is Damien."

"Damien, how are you? I didn't think you were going to call."

"I had some business to take care of, and then I had to run a few errands for my co-workers. You know how that goes…anyway, what have you been up to today?"

"Oh, nothing much. We laid out on the beach for a little while, and then we went to the bistro for a few drinks, that's about it."

"Sounds like you were on chill mode. Look Cindy, I hate to be so forward, but I really want to see you again before I leave; can I pick you up?"

"What do you have planned?" Cindy was picking Damien for information. She wanted to see where his mind was, to see if what Leslie told her was true.

"I wanted to get something to eat, go for a walk on the beach, talk under the moonlight, and let fate handle the rest."

"So, you're superstitious?" Cindy said, as she laughed into the phone's receiver.

"No, not really. It's just that some things happen, and some things are just meant to be. I mean, out of all of the people that live on this planet, why did WE meet each other yesterday in the middle of nowhere? It must have been meant to be, right?"

"Right, Damien. Anyway, I have a plan of my own. How about we skip the beach, and I bring YOU dinner. I wouldn't mind meeting your co-workers. I mean, if it's meant to be, then they will eventually know who I am anyway, right?"

Damn she's good, Damien thought to himself. *And all this time, I thought white girls were easy.*

"Okay, that sounds good. You got some paper to write down the directions?"

"Directions? I know this island like the back of my hand. I've been coming here with Brooke since my sophomore year at Florida State. Which beach house is it?"

"We're at the Tempest, on Paradise Lane."

"Oooh, that's a nice one. I need to take a bath and make sure Brooke and the rest of the girls are okay first, so give me a couple of hours; let's say around nine o'clock."

"That sounds good. I'll see you then, okay?"

"Okay, bye."

"Bye." Damien hung up the phone, smiled, and while holding a clutched fist, emitted a satisfying and familiar sound of conquest.

"Yesss."

*   *   *

The game was nearing halftime by the time Damien emerged from the stairwell. Antoine and Kym had returned from their walk, and were talking to Felicia and drinking water in the kitchen. Kelvin was leaning forward on the loveseat, boisterous as usual, talking to the television as if the players on the court could hear his every word.

"Take it to him Bibby, take it to him!"

"What's the score?" Damien interjected, as he took a seat in the wicker chair.

"Forty-five, thirty-eight, Kings."

"We'll be winning by twenty in the fourth, you know how we do it," Damien taunted, trying to disrupt Kelvin's concentration.

"Whatever, man, just relax and watch the Wolves take this ass whupping."

Just as Damien got settled in, the front door opened. It was Stacey and Leslie. They came in laughing and giggling like Nettie and Celie from *The Color Purple*.

"Hi, guys," Stacey called out, as she turned the corner and headed towards the room she was sharing with Kym.

"Hey, ladies," Damien said.

"Hey, girls. Did you enjoy the island?" Felicia asked.

"Yes!" Leslie said enthusiastically. "We went to the park, and it was absolutely beautiful! We even crashed a family reunion; they came down from Montgomery for the weekend to enjoy the beach and to have a cookout."

"Did they feed you?" Antoine asked.

"They offered, but we didn't want to be rude; we did try some sweet potato pie, though. It was delicious!"

"Good! It sounds like you two had a blast," Felicia said.

"We did, Felicia; believe me, we did." Leslie glanced at Damien with a sly smile, and headed towards the stairwell. Her eyes were piercing, sharp, and cold-blooded. Her last sentence seemed to linger in the air as if it had been projected through an echo chamber. He could sense that Leslie had something on her mind; he was trying to figure her out, but he couldn't. She said a few more words, and continued on her mission.

"I'll be back up in a minute; I need to take a quick shower."

"Okay, but don't be too long; hot pizza is on the way," Felicia said.

"Okay," Leslie said, as she disappeared down into the depths of the Tempest.

Leslie was beginning to savor her plan for revenge on Damien. Co-workers or not, she felt betrayed when he allowed his drunken alter ego to overpower his common sense. She felt weak and powerless, less than a woman. And now it was time for her to exact some measure of justice on the sly fox that had invaded her personal space.

Yeah, Leslie thought to herself. *You think you've got it made. You think you can just conquer any female you get your hands on, and she is just supposed to take it as it comes, huh? Well, Mister Damien Harris, you've got another thing coming. I'm going to show you that you screwed up. This time, you got the right one, baby. And now you've got hell to pay. That's right, you bastard. I'm gonna get you for the old AND the new.*

Leslie went into her room, gathered her toiletries and a change of casual clothes, and headed towards the bathroom. It was only a matter of time before Damien would know what Leslie had in store for him; she was feeling more excited by the moment, and wondered if Damien could sense the imminent danger that lie ahead.

*   *   *

Antoine was in the kitchen talking with Kym and Felicia about the marketing project, but his mind was almost four hundred miles away. It seemed like the closer he and Shauna came to finalizing their wedding plans, the more anxious she was becoming. *I shouldn't be rushing her into this,* he thought. *I didn't even consider her parent's reaction to us moving in together before we got married. If the fellowship at Wings of Grace finds out about this, we won't ever live this down. Here we are, the perfect couple, with so much to gain; yet I feel nervous, like I could lose everything I've worked for, before I can enjoy any of it. I need to call Shauna and apologize for acting irrationally, and tell her to take her condo off the market. I want our wedding to be perfect; I don't want anything or anyone to destroy this blessed union. I have finally found the perfect woman, in mind, body, and spirit.*

As soon as he started to excuse himself to the sitting room, his conversation with Kym began to replay in his mind. During their walk, a conversation had ignited about relationships; Antoine asked Kym if she thought it was possible for two people to love each other with the exact same passion and intensity. Kym's opinion was that one person in a relationship would always love the other a little more, even if the amount were miniscule. The key, in her mind, was that the other person recognize that deficit and FIND a way to love their partner a little more. Antoine was beginning to realize that he was suffocating his woman with love. There was no way he could force Shauna to love him, no matter how many shopping excursions or weekend trips he provided. He decided right then that he needed to back off, and let their relationship run its course. For months, he had been parading Shauna around as if she were a Super Bowl trophy. It was time for him to grow up and let their love blossom, without artificial influence.

Instead of calling Shauna, Antoine decided to give his phone a rest. He was determined to go back to Atlanta with a different attitude.

"Antoine?" Felicia asked, as she put her hand on his elbow to shake him out of his trance.

"Are you alright?"

"Yeah, yeah, I'm fine. I just have a lot on my mind, that's all." Antoine adjusted his eyes back into reality, and let the sights and sounds of the beach house reenter his conscience. His soft brown eyes had been transfixed on the black microwave above the stove for about three minutes, staring right through Felicia and Kym as if they were glass figurines. He saw their mouths moving, but their conversation had become a blur. He moved his left hand from the kitchen counter, uncrossed his legs, and brushed the crinkles out of his shirt. He pushed the power-off button on his cell phone, and decided to enjoy the rest of the night with his co-workers. After he readjusted, his attention was immediately grabbed by the playful in game arguing between Kevin and Damien. Kelvin's high-decibel couch cheerleading was so annoying to Antoine, that he wondered silently what

Kelvin could possibly do to make Felicia love him the way she does. *There is obviously some kind of educational gap there,* he thought to himself. *He's not even on her level socially. I would pay a thousand dollars to know how a woman as ambitious as her could love a loser like Kelvin.* Before he could find a rational answer, a few loud knocks creased the warm, evening air.

"I got it!" Stacey yelled, as the warm, humid mist rolled from the confines of the foyer bathroom. She opened the bathroom door, took a few steps to her right, and reached for the doorknob. Her head was still covered with a plastic hair protector, her face lacked mascara, and her pink house shoes did not match the long, power blue t-shirt that almost covered most of her knees. For the first time, she looked like a mortal. She turned the doorknob, and her eyebrows immediately rose with concern. The pizza delivery driver looked like the stepson of a Hells Angels bike rider. A few of his teeth from the top and bottom row were completely misplaced, his hair looked greasy and unkept, and the pizza boxes were not in a protective warmer. He wore an old t-shirt that read *White Zombie* with a faded image of a human skull below the name of the rock band. He looked to be in his early twenties, a sign that he probably was a loser in life, as demonstrated by the putt-putt sound the muffler on his AMC Gremlin emitted within a few feet of the front door.

"Pizza maaim," the deliveryman said, as Stacey frowned upon his disheveled frame. She hesitated for a moment, and then called for Felicia to settle the bill. Felicia grabbed her purse from the room, walked to the front door, and extracted some money from the white bank envelope that lay underneath her house keys, lipstick, earrings, phone numbers from church, and a few other assorted knick-knacks that contributed to the clutter in her purse.

"That'll be twenty-seven thirty-two," the delivery driver said. Felicia looked at the delivery driver with concern, motioned to Stacey to take the three large pizzas, gave him two crisp new twenty-dollar bills, smiled, and closed the door. Stacey walked a few steps, and turned to wait for Felicia.

"Do you know what you gave him?" Stacey asked Felicia, over the fading hum of the loud car muffler and the excitement of the basketball game.

"I sure do," Felicia responded calmly, as she turned the front door lock and headed towards Stacey. "You never know what a simple gesture like that can do to brighten up someone's day. Plus, he's probably been told all of his life that black folks don't tip."

Stacey cracked a light smile, shrugged her shoulders, and headed towards the kitchen.

"Ooooh!" Damien exclaimed loudly. He was rocking back and forth on the wicker chair with his fist covering his mouth, causing it to squeak. Kevin Garnett had just power-slammed a dunk for two points to give the Timberwolves a one-point lead over their new archrivals. As the excited commentators broke down the Kings' defensive flaws repeatedly during several instant replays, Kelvin held steadfast in his belief that they would shatter the Wolves' confidence by winning with a last-second shot.

"Watch this, Damien," Kelvin proclaimed. "Their defense can't stop the three-point play. It's do-or-die, baby! Four seconds in the game! Let's go, Folk!"

"It's over, man," Damien responded coolly. "We got 'em right where we want 'em." After a quick television timeout, the game's best drama was set to unfold.

"Alright, Kings," Kelvin said, as he rubbed the palms of his hands together nervously.

Damien sat up in the chair, displaying a nervous smile. The referee blew the whistle, and handed the ball to the Kings guard, Michael Bibby. He unsuccessfully looked for someone to inbound the ball to, and called the team's last timeout.

"See?" Damien said, as Kelvin let out a deep sigh. "I told you, they don't know what to do. We're covering them like glue on flypaper."

As Felicia and Stacey poured some ice into plastic cups for everyone, Kym and Antoine set the dining table with napkins and paper plates. The volume of the television, coupled with Kelvin and Damien's yelling were getting on Antoine's last nerves. He wanted badly to say something to them, but didn't want to spoil the rest of the evening by arguing with the two numbskulls. Leslie emerged from the staircase, looking refreshed and rejuvenated. She asked if there was anything she could do to help, but Felicia told her to just sit down and relax.

"Baby," Felicia called out to Kelvin.

"Yeah?" he said, over the din of the television commercials.

"Is the game almost over?"

"Yeah, in a few more seconds."

"Okay, the pizza is ready."

"Alright."

Damn, Kelvin thought to himself. *Do I look like a child? I know the damn pizza is ready, I can see it sitting over there. I can smell it too. Felicia's tripping with this mother-may-I routine she's pulling. Hell, I wish they could see her at the house during the week. She can hardly keep up with Jordan, much less school or church, or the book club, or any of that stuff. She's just trying to wear some pants that don't fit, that's all. Trying to play Superwoman in front of her co-workers. It's all right though. Let 'em think what they wanna think. I won't see none of 'em after tomorrow anyway. I'll be SO glad to get back to Atlanta.*

The last commercial faded, and the television cameras panned across a voracious, towel-waving crowd that was getting raucous with anticipation of the game's last play. The referee once again blew his whistle, and handed the ball to the Kings' all-star guard. He faked a throw left, then right, and executed a perfect push-pass to one his teammates. His teammate paused momentarily, threw an elbow at two Wolves defenders, and bounce-passed the ball back to the running Bibby, who dribbled once, took two steps towards the basket, and launched himself into the air, pushing a pump-shot over the outstretched arms of three defenders. As the ball sailed towards it's destination twelve feet away, Kelvin and Damien fell silent. Their eyes stretched as wide as saucers, and they held their breath like a pair of newborn infants. Damien sat forward in the wicker chair, gripping the sides tightly. Kelvin lurched forward off of the loveseat, positioning himself in a crouching pose, with his right knee and hand on the floor, and his left elbow secure on his left knee. The ball clipped the edge of the rim, bounced off of the backboard, and was quickly tipped back by the long, outstretched arm of a Kings player that emerged through the crowd of hungry gazelles. Swish! The crowd went wild.

"Yeah! Yeah! Yeah!" Kelvin yelled ecstatically, as he pumped his fist with joy. "I told you, Damien! Minnesota can't handle us. What? What you got to say now, huh?" Kelvin taunted Damien, looking for him to make an excuse.

"That's all right, Damien responded, with a dejected look on his face. "We've still got two more games, so I'm not worried about it."

"We'll see," Kelvin said. "I say we'll be in the Western Conference championship after Monday, and if we do, my bank account will be looking reeeal pretty."

Antoine shook his head at the childish acting pair of grown men, and helped Felicia and Stacey set the last few cups on the table.

* * *

14 Saturday Night

"Uuuuoohp!"

"Oh my God, Kelvin!" Felicia was taken aback and thoroughly embarrassed by Kelvin's selfish and disrespectful burp that emanated from his big, brown, juicy lips. Kelvin was sitting on the loveseat, soaking up the *SportsCenter* highlights, basking in the Kings' thrilling victory. He was obviously beginning to feel a little too comfortable in his new environment, even though he wasn't part of the official visit. While Antoine and the ladies ate pizza and waxed philosophic about how well the marketing plan would be received by the Convention and Visitor's Bureau, Kelvin and Damien had been dipping into the liquor stash. They were into their second glass of Hennessy and Coke, when Felicia intervened.

"Kelvin, come here for a minute please," Felicia requested sternly. She had stood up from the dining table and started walking towards the bedroom, pausing momentarily to motion for Kelvin with her right index finger. Kelvin looked back over his left shoulder in time to catch the cold, angry frown that was pasted onto Felicia's face. *Aww Hell,* Kelvin thought to himself, *Here we go...*

"Hey man," Kelvin said to Damien, "Hold it down for a minute; I'll be right back."

A smile cracked across Damien's lips, and he responded with a sly remark.

"Alright, B; whatever you say."

Damien snickered quietly, as Kelvin lumbered slowly towards Felicia, who stormed quietly into the bedroom like a midnight banshee.

Kelvin entered the bedroom to find Felicia standing in front of the queen bed with her arms folded. The two-socket ceiling light that flooded the room brightly illuminated the peach hue of the walls. The light cover was missing, causing Kelvin to squint like an international terrorist in a CIA interrogation room.

"Close the door Kelvin," Felicia said sternly.

"Damn Felicia," Kelvin responded with a slight slur. "Did you have to turn on that bright ass light? Why don't you cut on that lamp, instead?" Kelvin said, motioning towards the dresser. Felicia said nothing, and waited for the door to close. Before Kelvin took two steps, Felicia's nose was a pencil length away from Kelvin's face.

"Look Kelvin, enough is enough. I told you before we left Atlanta that the reason I invited you on this trip was so you wouldn't feel uncomfortable with me being at the beach for the weekend with my male co-workers. I've been trying to accommodate you and everybody else so this trip would be productive and fun at the same time. Now, it seems like you're doing your best to show your behind, and let everybody know who "THE MAN" is," Felicia said, using the index and middle fingers of both her hands to form moveable quotation marks, "like you're in a competition or something."

Felicia had finally reached her breaking point. She was tired of flip-flopping between the super-egotistical needs of Kelvin and Antoine. To her, it was childish and unnecessary. To them, however, it was a classic territorial battle between males. And in that kind of competition, there are no rules. Kelvin looked at

Felicia with slightly glazed eyes, as his body rocked carefully under the influence of alcohol. He laid his left arm across his stomach to support his right arm, which he used to caress his clean-shaven chin. The Hennessy was beginning to take effect, and he needed a few extra seconds to gather his thoughts.

"Well?" Felicia solicited a response, while inhaling the sweet, fermented odor on Kelvin's breath. Kelvin blinked his eyelids slowly a few times, and tried to make sense of the situation.

"You talking about the burp I just let out?

"YES, Kelvin. That was very rude and inappropriate. You're starting to act like you're at home or something."

"So, I ASKED to come on this trip, huh?" Kelvin responded sarcastically. He was beginning to go on the defensive.

"No, I already told you why I invited you," Felicia said.

"So basically, you really didn't want me to come on the trip; you just didn't want me to think you and 'ole boy were kicking it, huh?"

"Kelvin, what are you talking about? Kicking it with who?" Felicia took a step back, folded her arms, and promptly snapped her eyebrows up, looking for Kelvin to explain his position further.

"I see how Antoine has been acting towards you. He's been jealous of me since he got here. Hell, I'm your husband. I've been trying to be easy on him, give him some slack. I know ya'll talk at work. You're probably his confidant, huh? Just from the stuff you've told me about him, I know he thinks you're best friends, or something."

"It's not just that, Kelvin. You're also—"

"Also what? I just can't do right, can I Felicia?"

"Baby, all I'm saying is that you don't have to prove anything to my co-workers. Let's just relax, and enjoy the rest of the night, okay? The weekend is almost over, and we don't need to be upset with each other. Let's just have fun, and go home happy, okay?" Felicia stepped towards Kelvin, and made a motion to grab his hands. He refused, and turned towards the door.

"Kelvin, wait. I just want to—"

"Don't worry about it Felicia, I get the message." Kelvin opened the door and walked out, leaving Felicia standing alone feeling hurt and confused.

Kelvin went back to the living area to join Damien and watch the rest of *SportsCenter*.

Antoine, Leslie, Kym, and Stacey were still at the table, finishing their conversation and a few more slices of pizza.

"Like I said, I told you I'd be right back," Kelvin bragged to Damien.

"Yeah, yeah, whatever. So what's the plan for the rest of the night? I've got a hot date coming over in a little while," Damien said.

"Oh, really?" Kelvin said. "Felicia's probably got something planned, but I want to get a game of Questions going."

"Oh, snap," said Damien. "I played that a few times up at Central. If you have the right people, that game is fun as hell."

"I just like the fact that you can ask anything you want," Kelvin said. "We're gonna have some fun tonight."

Back in the room, Felicia sat at the foot of the bed, feeling somber. She wiped a lonely tear away from her left eye, and stared at the floor in deep thought. *All I wanted to do,* she thought, *was to come here, be productive, and keep everyone entertained. How in the world did it end up being like this? Why is Antoine playing head games with Kelvin? Why does Kelvin feel like he always has something to prove? Please, God, just let me get through the rest of this night without any more trials. Lord knows I'm tired. I've got too much on my plate to have anything else to worry about.* After a few more minutes of meditation, Felicia finally managed to regain her composure. She went into the bathroom, washed her face, and exited the bedroom to join the rest of her co-workers in the living area.

"So, what's up for tonight Felicia?" Leslie asked, anxious to get the party started. "I know you have something planned."

"Yeah, I'm ready to loosen up a bit," Antoine said.

"You won't hear any complaints here," Stacey added, as she smiled with a wide grin.

Kym just smiled in agreement, stood up, and headed towards the foyer bathroom to wash her hands.

"I thought we could relax a little bit, maybe play some Monopoly or something," Felicia said, as she picked up the white and red rectangular shaped box from its resting place next to the sofa.

"I got the car!" Damien exclaimed, overhearing Felicia's comment.

"I'll take the shoe!" Stacey said, as the game piece bidding got underway.

Antoine chose the hat, Felicia claimed the horse, and Leslie chose the plow. Leslie and Stacey cleared off the table, and Kym returned from the restroom, claiming the dog as her game piece. Felicia organized the money for distribution.

"You playing Kelvin?" Antoine asked, hoping his buddy would accept.

"Naw; ya'll go ahead and play. I'm straight." Felicia glanced over from the table to look at Kelvin, rolled her eyes, and let out a small sigh. She distributed the money to the players, and the game got underway. After thirty minutes of play, Damien began to worry about Cindy's whereabouts. He glanced at his wristwatch, and then at the wall clock above the television. They both read 8:33.

Twenty minutes later, Antoine emerged victorious, bankrupting everyone at the table.

"Ahh, the thrill of victory, the agony of defeat," Antoine gloated, as he thumbed through his pile of play money.

"Lucky dice rolls," Kym kidded.

"Yeah, yeah, whatever you say. Just make sure you see me on the first and fifteenth," Antoine shot back. Small laughter filled the room. Stacey and Leslie were giggling too; they were also ready to follow Damien and Kelvin's lead at the bar.

"C'mon girl, let's hit the kitchen. I'm ready to get loose," Stacey said.

"Let's do it," Leslie responded.

"Don't ch'all want me to beat up on you again?" Antoine asked, as they headed towards the kitchen.

"Hold your horses Kemosabe," Stacey said. "As a matter of fact," Leslie added, "You all go ahead and get started without us. We might be over here for a minute." They grabbed a few coolers out of the fridge, and headed out onto the deck to enjoy the warm Florida breeze, and the soothing sound of ocean waves spraying white sea foam against the evening shore. A few rays of light hung stubbornly onto the skyline, emitting a faint hue of orange, red, and yellow across the horizon. The smell of salty air permeated both sets of nostrils. Leslie took a seat in one of the white plastic lounge chairs that dotted the deck. Stacey quickly followed. As they untwisted the bottle tops from the Strawberry Daiquiri wine coolers, Stacey struck up an interesting topic of conversation.

"Leslie, what do you think about women who flirt to get ahead in their careers?"

Leslie glanced over at Stacey, took a sip from her cooler, and responded.

"To be honest with you, I was always taught to use my brains and integrity to scale the job ladder. However, working down South in this corporate environment has shown me that sometimes you have to utilize all of your weapons to reach your career goals. Why do you ask?"

"I was just curious about what women think of other women who do that in the office, because I see how male clients respond to the associates who show a little cleavage. I was taught in college to dress and act conservatively, and approach all business dealings with confidence and tact. But with the state of our economy, and the way folks are losing their jobs, sometimes I feel like I need an edge. Shoot, everybody knows the business. What's going to attract a client to you as opposed to the next person?" Stacey said.

"True," Leslie answered. "And you obviously have a beautiful package to work with," she said. She looked to her left, and scanned Stacey's body from head to toe. "However, you need to realize that if you make a conscious decision to use your body as a business tool, that the people you do business with might expect more than business from you."

"I know girl, I know." Stacey stared out into the darkness of the Gulf. She knew it would be risky to resort to using flirting tactics in her business dealings, because she knew she wasn't the type of girl to actually give up the goods unless she was genuinely attracted to her suitor. She also knew that it wouldn't be long before Concepts started distributing pink slips in earnest. The rumors had been swirling for months, and the word was, management would begin with the employees with the lowest client revenue. She had to do something, because client companies were cutting their operating costs, and the advertising budget was usually among the first to get slashed. She had already lost three clients in the last month, and her portfolio was shrinking fast. Her modeling gigs were beginning to pick up, but she couldn't count on those to pay the bills.

*   *   *

Antoine was working on his second victory in a row, when the doorbell rang.

"I wonder who that could that be?" Felicia said, prior to completing a real estate transaction with Antoine.

"I'll get it," Kym said, as she pushed her chair back from the dining table. Damien was hoping it was Cindy.

"Your roll Damien," Antoine said. He didn't want to pause game play. "All right," Damien responded. He picked up the dice, shook them loosely in his right hand, and let them spin across the Monopoly board.

Kym approached the front door with caution, peeking through the foyer window to see who their late night visitor was. *I wonder what SHE wants,* Kym thought to herself, as she moved her right hand towards the doorknob. She unlocked the door, and cracked it slightly to question the stranger.

"May I help you?" Kym asked, as she scanned the young woman's features into her short-term memory. *About five-five, close-cropped brunette, pretty and well-sculpted face, tanned skin, athletic shape, dressed in a white crochet tank top with black trim, black cotton skort with toe loop thong sandals, holding what appears to be a white carry-out bag from a restaurant in one hand, a purse, some keys, and a box of chocolates wrapped in red ribbon in the other.*

"Yes, I'm Cindy. I'm here to see Damien; am I at the right place?" Cindy could hear the chatter in the background, but sensed suspicion by the way Kym answered the door.

"Oh, okay," Kym said, looking surprised. "C'mon in." Kym closed the door behind the late night visitor, and guided her towards the activity.

"Hello," Cindy said as she stepped around the corner. Her tanned legs were highlighted by the track lighting above the dining room table. Damien had just advanced his game piece five spaces on the Monopoly board, landing on the chance space. *Damn,* Damien thought, as he glanced over at Cindy; *She looks better than she did last night. I'd better play this one right, or I may be sleeping alone tonight.*

Felicia and Antoine eyed the Caucasian visitor from head-to-toe, formulating instant opinions about her age, education, income level, and the reason why she was standing before them at this particular moment in time.

"Everyone, this is Cindy; we met yesterday. Cindy, these are my co-workers," Damien said, trying to break the tense atmosphere that was immediately created by her presence. He quickly stood up from the table and grabbed the plastic bag and chocolates from her hand, sneaking a quick hug in for good measure.

"Hi Cindy, I'm Felicia," Felicia said, and extended a cordial handshake. "Hello, my name is Antoine," Antoine said, as he turned and stood from his seat at the head of the table.

"My name is Kym. Kym Kersey," Kym said, with a slight, but friendly smile.

"Nice to meet you guys. Sorry to disturb your game of Monopoly; I just came over to—"

"No, no, make yourself right at home," Felicia said. "We just didn't know that anyone was going to be joining us tonight, that's all." Felicia's remark was accompanied by an icy stare directed towards Damien, as if she already knew his intentions. Kelvin was fast asleep on the sofa, and missed the formal introductions.

"What did you bring, Cindy? I really wasn't expecting anything you know," Damien asked, flattered by Cindy's generosity.

"I told you I would bring you dinner. It's from the Blue Parrot Café; some blackened shrimp and fried Grouper along with vegetables. I hope you eat seafood. The chocolates are for dessert."

Damien was blown away. For the first time in his life, he didn't have to do any work. This girl came to him, without fight nor fuss, and brought grade-A seafood and sweets to boot.

He was definitely impressed with her appearance. Her shapely hourglass figure looked like the silhouette of an Olympic tri-athlete, and her outfit was a perfect match. The silver necklace and diamond pendant she wore was an enticing invite to stare at her chest, and the anklet she wore highlighted her perfectly manicured toes, causing a chill to run down Damien's spine. As she stood there flashing a pearly-white smile, Damien stared, transfixed by Cindy's allure, taken aback by all that made her a woman. He stared deep into her cocoa brown, Italianesque eyes, and mustered enough strength to invite her downstairs.

"Why don't we go downstairs; it's a little more private down there. My stomach is killing me. I haven't eaten since early this afternoon."

"Okay," Cindy answered reluctantly. She wanted badly to ask where Leslie and Stacey were, but didn't want to give the real purpose of her visit away.

"You want something to drink?" Damien asked. "We've got wine coolers, martinis, dark liquor, and sodas." He was hoping she would choose the alcohol, of course, so he could launch a quick strike.

"I'll take a wine cooler," Cindy said, as she followed him towards the kitchen. Damien quickly grabbed a wine cooler out of the refrigerator, handed it to Cindy, and made a beeline towards the staircase. His Monopoly game was history.

"C'mon, follow me," Damien said, cocky and arrogant as ever. As they made the spiral descent, Damien's mind spun with wordplays that could get him into Cindy's panties. Cindy's mind was overloaded with methods of escape, just in case Damien tried anything funny.

"This is a nice beach house," Cindy remarked, making small talk. "Wow, a pool table too. I didn't know that was in here."

"Yeah, our boss likes to set it out," Damien responded coolly. "C'mon in here; we can watch TV while we eat." Damien turned the doorknob carefully, while trying to avoid tipping the plastic bag over. He placed the food on the bed, and the chocolates on the nightstand.

"Make yourself comfortable," Damien said, as he turned around to see that Cindy was leaning on the doorframe. She sat on the foot of the bed, placed her keys and purse on the floor, and opened her wine cooler while Damien turned on the television.

"Wow, looks like you got the best view," Cindy said, gazing across the moonlit beach as Damien joined her at the foot of the bed.

"That's the only way I roll baby," Damien said, as he opened his seafood dinner.

"You sure you want to eat that with all that white on?" Cindy asked, eyeing his thin linen and cotton outfit. She was beginning to have doubts about what Leslie told her earlier. Damien seemed nice to her, and he looked really sexy right about now. She was going to have to be reaffirmed in some manner if she was going to pull their stunt off as planned.

"Actually, I have a change of clothes in my bag if you don't mind me changing in front of you," Damien said, immediately testing his limits with Cindy.

"I have two brothers, so it won't be anything I haven't seen before," Cindy shot back. Damien smiled sheepishly, closed the food container, retrieved a thin pair of light blue denim shorts and a green Adidas t-shirt out of his travel bag, and began to undress.

*   *   *

"Girrl, I'm about ready for another cooler, how 'bout you?" Leslie said, as she and Stacey rambled about men, their careers, and the urban dating scene in Atlanta.

"Shit, I'm ready for a martini," Stacey said, ready to fully relax and enjoy the serenity that nature had provided. As the chirping and singing of the seagulls began to subside, Stacey wondered what happened to Cindy.

"I wonder what happened to Cindy? It's after nine-thirty."

"I don't know; maybe she chickened out. You think we should call her again?" Leslie asked.

"Nahh. If she doesn't show, we'll let human relations deal with him. Either way, he's going to get his."

"True, true. Anyway, enough of that; Let's go back inside and join the party. They're probably wondering what we're doing anyway," Leslie said. Stacey and Leslie stood up, picked up their empty bottles, and slid back inside to check on everyone else.

"We're baaack!" Stacey said, as they made their way to the liquor cabinet.

"It's just you three?" Leslie asked, as Felicia, Kym, and Antoine conversated over Kelvin's intermittent snores.

"Yeah, Kelvin is asleep, and Damien is downstairs with his date," Felicia said, as she nonchalantly returned to their conversation.

"Leslie turned towards Stacey, who heard Felicia's comments, and whispered "Oh, shit." Stacey's eyes were as wide as a doe, and she grabbed Leslie by the arm to emphasize her point.

"What are we going to do? They're down there by themselves. He could be raping her as we speak!" Stacey's tone was firm, but low. They didn't want to give away the secret happenings to everyone else and have Damien's business all over Concepts, not yet anyway. That would be a disaster, because then he might be able to sue for slander.

"Girl, let's go downstairs and pretend like I had to get something out of my room," Leslie suggested. "That sounds good," Stacey said, "but we need to play it cool. Let's fix some martinis and go down there like we don't even know she's here."

"Cool," Leslie said. They shook a set of apple martinis and some ice in a silver martini shaker, and poured them into plastic martini glasses. Then, they set off on their mission.

*   *   *

15 Saturday Night

"C'mon girl," Stacey said, as they crept down the stairs towards the recreation room. The entire area was dark, except for the moon's natural illumination that bounced gently off of the Gulf of Mexico in the distance, and the television light that flickered under the door to Damien's room.

"Damn, I hope it's not too late," Stacey said, as they paused next to the mini-bar to detect any conversation. Leslie crept a few feet closer towards the door, sliding her left hand along the side of the pool table as she went. As she caressed the wood and carpet-lined paneling with her left hand, she carefully knelt down near the front of the table and placed her martini on the floor, near her right side. She cocked her right ear towards Damien's room, and proceeded to spy upon their private interlude.

"Umm, that was sooo good," she heard Damien remark. *Damn, did she give it up THAT fast?* Leslie thought to herself. She leaned a little closer to see what she could hear. "Wait 'till you taste the dessert," a petite voice said, duplicating the voice Leslie heard on the phone earlier in the afternoon.

"Let's open it," Damien said. Leslie heard the same sense of urgency in his voice not twenty-four hours earlier. She hoped Cindy had sense enough to stall him out.

"Let's wait," Cindy said. "We've got all night for that. I don't want your co-workers to think I'm some kind of floozy. Let's go back upstairs for a little while, so I can get to know them; then, we can come back down here so I can get to know you." Damien's libido immediately went into overdrive.

"Let's go!" Leslie whispered, as she scrambled to her feet, spilling some of her martini on the floor in the process. As she and Stacey made a hurried dash towards her room, Damien's door popped open.

"Hey ladies!" Damien said, freezing them in their tracks.

"Whooo! You scared me, Damien," Stacey said, as she whipped her head around towards his voice. "We didn't know anyone was down here," Leslie said, taking her hand off her room's doorknob, trying to play it off.

"I'm sorry, I didn't mean to do that. Next time, I'll leave a note by the stairwell."

"Funny Damien, funny," Stacey responded. Cindy emerged from behind Damien with a half-empty wine cooler in her hand, and cracked a shy smile towards the meddling pair.

"Hi."

"Hello," Stacey and Leslie said, in almost perfect unison. They looked Cindy up and down, trying to match their preconceived notions of what she looked like with the real thing. From their earlier conversation, Leslie was expecting a stringy haired blonde, with small town looks. Instead, Cindy stood before them looking like a prowling tigress. *Wow, she's got a really nice shape,* Stacey thought to herself. *Umph; not bad for a white girl, not bad at all,* Leslie thought to herself.

"Allow me to introduce," Damien said. "Cindy, meet my co-workers Stacey and Leslie, Stacey and Leslie, this is Cindy."

"Hi Cindy," Stacey said, projecting her voice across the rec room.

"Nice to meet you," Leslie said. Cindy waved back at them, cracked a smile, and tapped Damien on the arm. "You ready?"

"Yeah, yeah. Come on, we'll see them upstairs," Damien said.

"You all coming back upstairs?" Damien asked the pair, as he and Cindy walked past the front of the pool table towards the stairwell.

"Yeah, we just had to get something out of Leslie's room, that's all," Stacey said.

"All right, see you in a minute," Damien said, and disappeared into the stairwell.

Leslie and Stacey looked at each other, let out heavy sighs of relief, and went into the room to catch their breath.

*   *   *

"Okay caveman, wake up," Damien commanded, as he shook Kelvin out of his sleep.

"Hey man, don't be runnin' up on me like that shawty; you liable to get knocked out," Kelvin said, trying to shake the cobwebs out of his head.

"Man, you gonna sleep the entire night, or what? I thought we were going to play Questions. I want my friend to see it," Damien said. Kelvin sat up with a frown on his face, and focused on the smiling white chick that sat staring at him from the loveseat.

"Kelvin, this is Cindy, Cindy this is Kelvin, Felicia's husband," Damien said.

"Hey, how you doing," Kelvin said, skipping the formal handshake to wipe the sleep off of his face.

"Hi," Cindy replied, and placed her cooler on the table.

"Any of you all want something to drink? Damien asked, directing his attention to the dining table.

"What's in there?" Kym said.

"Sodas, coolers, Hennessy, martinis, and bottled water."

"I'll take a cooler," Kym said.

"I'll take the same," Antoine said.

"I'll take a bottled water please," Felicia answered. Damien went to retrieve the beverages from the kitchen, while Kelvin went to the room to wash his face. As the voices of Leslie and Stacey echoed from the bottom of the stairwell, Cindy glanced at the round, brown wall clock above the television. It read 10:03.

* * *

16 Saturday Night

"Alright everybody, listen up!" Damien yelled out over the small conversations.

"There's no way we're gonna sit here for the rest of the night like we're at happy hour for geriatrics. We're gonna play a game that Kelvin and I like called Questions; you all familiar with it?"

"Oh lord," Antoine said, slapping his forehead with his open right hand.

"What?" Damien asked Antoine.

"We played that game all the time on band trips. That can get folks in trouble," he said.

"Nah, not tonight. Tonight, it's all in fun. You playing ladies?" Damien said, as he looked at Leslie and Stacey standing in the kitchen.

"Yeah, we'll play," Stacey said, while taking a sip from her second martini.

"Felicia? Kym? You two playing?" Damien asked. He didn't want to leave anyone out.

"No thanks; I think I'll watch," Felicia said, declining the offer.

"Sure, why not?" Kym responded. "I've never played before, but it sounds fun."

"Cindy? You playing?" Damien was hoping she would, so he could find out how kinky she was.

"No thanks, I think I'll watch with Felicia," she said.

"Alright; did anybody bring a radio? The TV has to be off, so no one will lose their concentration, but soft music is okay," Damien said.

"I brought one," Kelvin said. "I've got some Al Green, O'Jays, Earth, Wind, and Fire, R. Kelly, Rick James, Ying Yang Twins, and Lil' John. I brought some old school mix CD's too."

They settled on one of the mix CD's, and listened to Damien explain the rules. "Okay, here are the rules. First, you must answer a question with a question. If you don't, you're automatically out of that round. Second, you have to look the person you're asking a question to straight in the eyes, so nobody will be confused about who you are talking too…"

"Can you finger point?" Leslie asked, out of curiosity.

"No, no you can't," Damien said. "People next to you in the circle might get confused about who you're pointing at. You MUST make direct eye contact, that's why everyone has to pay attention. Also, any pause over two seconds after you've been asked a question disqualifies you for that round."

"What kind of questions do you ask?" Kym said, still confused about the rules.

"Glad you asked," said Damien. "That's what makes this game so fun. You can ask anything you want, which brings me to the most important rule of all," Damien said, lifting his arms like a choir director. "What goes on in the game, STAYS IN THE GAME," everyone echoed, and fell out in laughter.

"One more thing," Kym said. "Are there rewards and punishments for this game?"

"Well, that depends on who you play with," Damien said. "We won't play with punishments tonight, besides making you blush with embarrassment, but I tell you what. The first person to win three rounds gets a twenty-five dollar gift certificate to the restaurant of their choice when we get back to Atlanta; that's five dollars from each of the losers."

"Alright, bet!" Kelvin said excitedly. "Let's do it!"

"Sounds good to me," Stacey said, with Leslie nodding her approval. Antoine and Kym agreed as well, and the game was underway. Felicia and Cindy settled down at the dining table; Damien sat in the wicker chair, Antoine parked in the loveseat, Stacey and Leslie sat on the sofa next to Kelvin, and Kym sat with her legs crossed on the floor between the couch and the television.

"Okay, I'll start out," Damien said. "Kym; you wanna watch us do a practice round, so you can get a hang of how to play?" he asked, turning his attention towards her.

"Sure, I'll watch," she said, picking her cooler up to take a sip. Kelvin twiddled his fingers with anticipation. He had a lot of questions in his mind, and now was the perfect time for them to be asked. Antoine was forming pre-planned questions as well, just in case the game turned personal. *Don't go there; please don't go there,* he thought to himself, referring his thoughts towards Kelvin. *I know a lot about you, more than you think.* Kelvin was thinking the same thing.

"Alright, here we go," Damien said. He sat up in the chair, causing the wicker to squeak. He scanned the circle going clockwise, trying to intimidate the competition. When he got to Leslie, he blinked. *I hope she doesn't say anything stupid about last night,* he thought to himself. *Don't worry lover boy,* Leslie thought, *your payback is coming later.* Damien looked to Leslie's right, and shot the first question at Kelvin.

"Are the Kings sorry?"

Kelvin stared Damien in the eyes and immediately returned the volley.

"Are the Timberwolves gonna be watching the championship from home?"

Damien quickly turned his attention towards Stacey.

"Are you wearing a thong?"

Stacey looked to her left at Leslie.

"Is that all he can think of?"

Leslie eyeballed Antoine.

"Do you REALLY want to get married?"

Antoine looked at Damien.

"What does Adidas stand for?"

Damien looked down at his shirt, and froze.

"AAH, HAA!" Stacey said, and the room burst out in laughter.

"Well, where I'm from, it means "All Day I Dream About Sex," Kelvin said, slapping his knee in laughter. Damien laughed at himself, and wondered what Adidas really stood for.

"Actually, Adidas is a blend of the first and last name of the company's founder, Adolph Dassler," Antoine said.

"And how do you know that?" Damien asked.

"Because I had the privilege of marketing their brand for three months during my college internship, that's how," Antoine smartly replied.

"Wow," Kym interrupted. "This game is cut-throat. I don't know if I can handle it."

"You'll be alright, girl," Leslie said. "You just have to think on your feet, that's all."

Damien turned towards Cindy, and mouthed the words "You alright?" She responded with a smile and a head nod, switched her crossed legs, and repositioned her folded arms.

"Okay, here we go. This round counts. Antoine, you got me out; you wanna start this one out?"

"Sure, no problem," Antoine said. He pulled from his curiosity bank, and went to work. He started out by testing Kym.

"What's your name?" he asked, looking her dead in the eye. She almost answered, because he caught her off guard, but she only paused momentarily before focusing on Kelvin.

"Did you sleep well?"

Kelvin returned the volley.

"Did your cigarettes taste good?"

Kym frowned, and turned quickly towards Damien.

"Where did you meet your friend?"

Damien paused briefly before asking the next question.

"Would you ride on a donkey to work?" Damien said to Antoine, whipping his head to the left, with a serious look.

"Do you go to church with your family?" Antoine said, looking Kelvin dead in the eyes.

No, no he didn't, Kelvin thought. He managed to keep his calm, sit forward, look to his right, and shoot Stacey a prefabricated question in less than a second.

"Is that a weave?"

Stacey quickly looked at Leslie.

"Does it matter what I wear in my hair?"

"Are you conceited?" Leslie said to Antoine.

"Are you the boss of me?" Antoine said, as he stared at Kym.

The deeper into the round they got, the funnier the questions became. Felicia, however, was catching a bad vibe. She knew her husband like the back of her hand, and Antoine's question about church was out of bounds. She could tell by Kelvin's body language that he was ready to strike back. The look in his eyes told her that he was prepared to wage war. She just hoped that nothing she'd told him about Antoine would come back to bite her.

After ten minutes or so, everyone had been eliminated except Damien and Stacey. They squared off in the fastest and most exciting part of a game of Questions, the two-person elimination. After a few witty and ferocious rapid fire exchanges, Damien went for the jugular.

"You think you're a pretty boy?" Stacey said. All eyes were on the dueling pair. Silence and smiles ruled the room.

"You think you're a pretty girl?" Damien shot back.

"Why are you wearing seventies sideburns?" Stacey said, causing Leslie and Kelvin to snicker.

"Are you a freak?" Damien said, trying to break her concentration.

"Is your momma a freak?" Stacey shot back, rolling her head for emphasis. She sat forward, placing her elbows on her knees. She had learned to intimidate opponents at the AU that way, but that didn't faze Damien.

"What'd you say?" Damien asked Stacey, with a serious frown on his face.

"I said, is your momma a FREAK?" Stacey repeated, putting emphasis on the word freak.

"Ahh haa! You're out," Damien said with glee. "You can't start a question with a statement, and you can't ask the same question twice in a row. Nahh!"

Everyone burst out into laughter, and Stacey threw her hands up in defeat. "You got me, pretty boy, you got me." Damien smiled across at Stacey, and made a suggestion.

"Ten minute break everybody. I think I need to fix another drink."

"That's what I'm talking about," Kelvin said. Kym let her legs out to stretch, and Leslie headed for the restroom. Stacey heard one of her favorite old school songs playing on the CD, and asked Felicia to turn it up.

Hoo! This stuff is starting now, it's the same feeling I always seem to get around you

There's no mistaking, I'm clearly taken by the simple mere thought of you...

As Stacey began to snap her fingers and twist her hips and torso in perfect rhythm, Damien and Kelvin acted like a pair of backup singers to Larry Blackmon. "This stuff is starting now, this stuff is starting now, this stuff is starting now, hoo!" they sung, while Damien reminisced about neighborhood basement parties in Cleveland back in the day.

Antoine's thoughts turned to Shauna, and his heart immediately fell ill. He missed her so much, he felt like he could run all the way back to Atlanta. He wanted badly to call her, so bad that his body began to rock with anticipation. *Be cool Antoine, be cool,* he thought. He stood up to get some fresh air outside, and met Felicia's cold stare instead. She didn't say a word, but from her look, he assumed that she wasn't happy about his question to Kelvin about going to church. She and Antoine had the discussion a few weeks ago at Concepts, and she told him to keep it to himself. He avoided prolonged eye contact, and headed towards the door.

*   *   *

After two more songs, Damien cut the music down and called the second round to order. Everyone took their places, and waited for Damien to issue the first question.

"Alright, here we go. Where were you born?" he asked Kym.

"Is that your business?" she shot back.

"You got good credit?" Damien said to Leslie, playing it safe. She wasn't about to get him caught up. Not tonight.

Leslie looked at Kelvin. "Is Damien shallow?" she said, hoping he would answer.

"What're you mixed with?" Kelvin asked Kym.

"Would that question be admissible in court?" Kym asked Stacey.

"Does the Marching One Hundred have one hundred marchers?" Stacey asked Antoine, trying to make him slip. After a few minutes, Damien and Kym were eliminated, leaving Kelvin, Leslie, Stacey, and Antoine. Damien allowed Stacey to take the wicker chair, and he sat at the dining table next to Cindy. Leslie had eliminated Damien by asking him if he was going to introduce Cindy to his mom. He was so embarrassed that he just covered his eyes with his hands, laughed, and shook his head. It was Leslie's turn to ask a question; she decided to start with Stacey.

"Where are all the good men?" Leslie asked. Stacey paused momentarily, but managed to get her question out.

"Did you walk on the beach today?" she asked Antoine. Antoine quickly turned to Leslie.

"Why aren't YOU married?" he said, trying to get her back from the first round. Leslie looked to her left, and deferred to Kelvin.

"Is marriage all it's cracked up to be?" In less than a millisecond, Felicia and Antoine's buddy-buddy relationship flashed through Kelvin's mind. In less than twenty-four hours, his hatred for him had increased ten-fold. He had taken Antoine's verbal jabs personally, and now it was payback time. He looked directly at Antoine, and went to work.

"Are you soft?" Kelvin said. Antoine frowned, and shot back at Kelvin.

"Are you too old to be wearing an Underground Atlanta t-shirt?" Kelvin's face twisted, and he leaned forward as the next question sailed off of his lips.

"Is your little toenail missing?" Kelvin said. He looked down at Antoine's sandal-covered feet, causing the pressure in Antoine's brain to boil. They were engaged in an all out Questions battle, a two-person elimination bout, without regard to the other players. Leslie sat back on the sofa, to avoid being hit by Kelvin's spittle, and Stacey sat up in the wicker chair with wide-open eyes. Felicia wanted badly to interrupt the game, but it was happening so fast, it seemed like a blur.

"Do you have a college degree?" Antoine shot back, as his eyes widened with fury. Felicia had heard enough, and tried to open her mouth as she stood up, but it was too late. Kelvin shot up from the couch, and fired off a question to Antoine that moved from his lips like fire.

"Can you tell us what it was like to tongue that nigga in college?"

Before he realized it, Antoine was lunging towards Kelvin, fists cupped, with full intentions of knocking his head off. Antoine had been exposed, his dark secret revealed. During his freshman year of college, his roommate's financial aid had dried up. He could no longer afford the expensive housing and out-of-state tuition fees, and had to return to Detroit. The next roommate was affable, and a favorite to sit near in class. When he complained to Antoine that he needed a new roommate, Antoine did not hesitate to volunteer his old roommate's vacant spot. They participated in study groups together, talked to girls on the set together, and played on Spades teams together in the dorm lobby.

Antoine had no idea about his roommate's bi-sexual lifestyle, until they bought some cheap wine one night, and went back to the room to get drunk. It was mid-summer, and Antoine's grandmother had just died. The dorms were mostly empty, except for some high school seniors who were involved in a summer band camp, a few summer school students, and some athletes. When he returned from Miami, he was emotionally drained. He had buried his grandfather less than two years prior, and needed someone to console him. Once the alcohol took full effect, Antoine began to cry, and his roommate took him on his shoulder. They were sitting on Antoine's bed, with a *Married...With Children* rerun playing silently on the small TV.

His roommate held the back of his head, and told him that everything was going to be okay. He lifted Antoine's chin with one hand, and wiped his tears away with the other. They looked each other in the eyes, and drew closer to each other until their lips touched. In an instant, their warm tongues probed slowly in each other's mouths, exchanging passionate, wine flavored saliva. His roommate's hand slid down the side of Antoine's torso, until it found a growing bulge in the front of his white shorts. When he began to rub, Antoine panicked. He separated himself from his roommate's embrace, pushed him back on the bed, asked him what he was doing, and kicked him out in an angry panic. He gathered his roommate's belongings, and placed them in the hallway before sunrise.

The only person in the world he had ever revealed this incident to was Felicia, the one person he felt he could trust with his deepest feelings and personal secrets. Antoine failed to assume however, that Felicia's conscience would eventually compel her to unload her workplace baggage onto Kelvin. Antoine's secret had been eating at her insides for quite some time. When she finally told Kelvin, she was trying to rid herself of the guilt she felt for telling their martial business to Antoine. Felicia tried her best to avoid this confrontation, but the seeds had already been sown.

BLAMM! The oak cocktail table crushed under the weight of the pair, as Kelvin tackled Antoine in mid-stride. Stacey's plastic martini glass spewed its liquid contents onto the floor between the wicker chair and the loveseat, and tumbled towards Felicia's screams. Damien instinctively leaped from his seat at the dining table, and ran towards the fracas.

"KELVIN!! STOP! OH GOD!" Felicia screamed, as she watched helplessly. Stacey slid the wicker chair back with her feet, and sat wide-eyed, in the fetal position. The faces of Leslie, Cindy, and Kym all displayed varying degrees of shock, but Leslie's voice was the only one besides Felicia's that was audible.

"Oh shit! Oh shit!" she said, as she retreated to the far corner of the couch. Antoine's feet kicked at Kelvin from the tangled mess, as he struggled to gain his bearings. Kelvin grunted, as he launched wild blows with his large fists, trying to connect with Antoine's head.

"Umph! Umph! Motherfff.......ucker!" Kelvin said, as he leaned down to grab Antoine's shirt with one hand, and swing with the other. At least three blows found their target before Damien could separate them. He snatched Kelvin's swinging arm in mid-air, and pulled it back, grabbing him around the waist for leverage. He screamed at Kelvin to chill out, and pushed him towards the sliding glass door. Kelvin continued to curse Antoine, between heavy gulps for air.

Antoine managed to stand up with Leslie and Felicia's assistance, and wipe the crimson blood that trickled from his bottom lip onto his mangled, sixty-dollar Versace shirt.

"Antoine, are you okay?" Felicia said, as she placed her hand on his arm.

"You know what, Felicia? The only reason I'm not pressing charges is because he's your husband. I can't believe you Felicia... I can't believe you," Antoine said, shaking his head in disgust. He pulled his arm away from Felicia's grip, and sped towards the kitchen. He darted into the stairwell, and disappeared without a sound.

"Hey man, you straight?" Damien said, as Kelvin sucked oxygen from the warm, salty air. Kelvin bent over with his hands on his knees, and threw up, causing Damien to jump backwards.

"Damn, man!" Damien said, narrowly escaping Kelvin's nervous reaction. Kelvin regained his balance, wiped his mouth, and spoke.

"Yeah, I'm straight; I'll be aiight. Hell, if it wasn't for you, I would have killed that punk." Kelvin leaned on the wall, using his right hand for support.

"Is that true what you said?" Damien inquired, wanting to know if Kelvin was serious.

"Yeah man, that's what Felicia told me. He kept trying me, folk. Wasn't no way I was gonna let him keep trying me like that. And if he says something smart out of his mouth again, I'll do the same thang." Damien wanted to laugh, but held his composure. *Antoine is gay?* he thought to himself. He let out a slight chuckle, and looked out towards the Gulf.

"You need some ice for your face?" Damien asked, referring to several scratches that Antoine inflicted just below Kelvin's left eye and on his forehead.

"Naw, I'm straight," Kelvin said. Just then, the sliding glass door opened. The look on Felicia's face told Damien that it was time to go back inside. She pulled the door closed behind Damien, and assessed her husband for damage.

"Kelvin, let me see your face." Kelvin turned around, resting his back on the wall. With his shoulders slouched, he brought his eyes up to meet Felicia's.

"Oh Jesus," she said, skipping to her right. She narrowly missed his puddle of vomit, whose odor was partly masked by the salty air. She placed her hands on his face, and moved it slowly from one side to the other.

Kelvin's eyes darted away from Felicia's stare. He suddenly felt like a jackass for not being able to control his anger. He didn't give a shit about Antoine, but he knew Felicia must have felt terribly embarrassed having to watch her husband fight Antoine right in front of everybody.

"Kelvin, look at me," she said. He avoided eye contact, and stared towards the gulf.

"KELVIN," she said, shaking his arms lightly at the wrists.

"Yeah," he replied softly. He finally rolled his eyes towards Felicia's tired face.

"Kelvin, it wasn't your fault," she said, expressing sincerity and concern. "The game just got out of hand. I tried to stop it, but it was too late. He attacked you first, Kelvin. I don't blame you for protecting yourself, Kelvin. I just wish you all would've handled it in a different way."

"Like what, Felicia?" Kelvin said. "I ain't gonna let nobody rush me like that and get away with it."

"I don't know," Felicia said. "I just know that we have a son to raise, and that's more important than anybody or anything in this world. I know how you carry your pride, but I don't ever want our family to be jeopardized because of somebody else's ignorance. You and Jordan are why I wake up every morning, and I don't ever want to lose either one of you."

Felicia pulled herself towards Kelvin, pressed her chest against his, and squeezed tight. For a minute, the sound of white-capped waves rolling gently against the shoreline replaced their conversation. As she felt Kelvin's heart return to its normal pace, Felicia's thoughts turned to the welfare of her co-workers. She knew she needed to diffuse any anxiety that lingered inside the house, and quick. She tightened her squeeze momentarily, and then released her grip. As she stepped back, Kelvin placed his hands on her forearms and gazed into her misty eyes.

"So what's up now?" Kelvin asked.

"Kelvin, don't get mad, but you have to do something."

"What?" Kelvin asked, in a curious, demanding tone.

"I need you to apologize."

"I'm not apologizing to that ni—"

"Aah, aah," Felicia interrupted, placing her index finger on his lips to lower his voice. "Not him, THEM," she continued, as she motioned with her head towards the living area. Felicia grabbed Kelvin by the hand and tugged his body towards the sliding glass door, despite his groaning protests. Once inside, Kelvin reluctantly garnered everyone's attention.

"Excuse me; I'm very sorry, everybody. I didn't mean to mess the night up and tear up the house like this. Whatever I have to pay for, I'll pay for," Kelvin announced.

Leslie and Stacey accepted Kelvin's apology, while Kym sat expressionless, staring at the physical aftermath in disbelief. Damien tossed his cup and Cindy's bottle in the trash, and led her back downstairs. He had seen enough drama in the living area. Plus, it was time for dessert.

Kym got up, said goodnight to everyone, and headed to her room to catch some much needed rest. Kelvin and Felicia did the same, leaving Stacey and Leslie to pick up the mess.

"Girrl, let's clean up," Leslie said, as Stacey shook her head. They were both speechless, but thankful for the late night entertainment. They quickly cleaned up the broken table, picked up Stacey's martini glass, wiped up the liquor that spilled on the floor, and put the half-empty pizza boxes into a black trash bag. Then, they headed downstairs to catch the finale.

*   *   *

17 Saturday Night

Leslie and Stacey reached the bottom of the stairs just as Antoine exited the bathroom. He had taken a long, hot shower, and was headed towards his sleeping quarters.

"Antoine, I—"

"Goodnight," a melancholy Antoine responded, cutting Leslie off. He wiped the excess dampness from his head with his towel, and followed his feet with his eyes. His silk pajamas were a far cry from the bloody, tattered outfit that had adorned his body minutes earlier. The only evidence that remained from his fight with Kelvin was a swollen bottom lip, and a growing knot that rested above his left temple. Antoine walked past them and into his room, closing the door, and turning the lock. Leslie looked at Stacey, raised her left eyebrow with resignation, and made her way towards her room. Stacey followed, curious to see if Cindy would follow through with the plan.

"Girl, do you think she's going to do it?" Stacey asked, plopping down on Leslie's bed.

"I don't know," Leslie said. She pulled her cell phone out of her purse, and waited for it to ring.

*   *   *

"Cindy, let's skip the chocolates," Damien said, eager to get into her panties. They had been kissing and rubbing each other for a few minutes, and Damien felt like he was about to explode. It had taken him seven minutes to explain the stupidity of Kelvin and Antoine to Cindy, and another five of ultra-smooth player talk to get her back into the mood. Now that she was hot, he wanted to skip the foreplay and get down to business.

"Slow down, soldier," Cindy replied. "Don't rush this," she said, placing her index finger on his lips. She sat up, reached for the box of chocolates on the nightstand, and slowly unwrapped it, seducing Damien with her eyes. She reached for a round chocolate with a flat bottom. She swirled the chocolate, which fit snugly between her thumb and index finger, towards Damien's mouth, teasing his taste buds. He opened his lips, closed his eyes, and received his prize with glee.

"Mmmm," Damien said, as he bit through the chocolate shell, releasing the creamy mandarin orange and butter crème filling. Cindy handed Damien a similar looking piece of chocolate, which he used to feed her, duplicating her finger dance. She took half of it into her mouth, and eased towards Damien, coaxing him to bite the other half. He touched her lips with his, and bit down on the chocolate, chewing and kissing at the same time. Cindy swallowed her half of the chocolate, and eased away from Damien's lips. She reached for a square chocolate this time, and pushed it through Damien's waiting lips. He chewed slowly, carefully digesting the solid square into a soft, liquid state. He pushed the chocolate back towards his throat, and swallowed. Before he could wrap his lips around Cindy's lips again, her cell phone rang.

"Damn," Damien said, out of frustration. "Don't answer it," he said, hoping that she would comply.

"Hold on, it might be Brooke," Cindy said, and reached for her purse at the foot of the bed. She unsnapped it, and grabbed her ringing cell phone.

"Hello?" she said, holding her free hand close to the receiver.

"Cindy, are you okay?" Leslie whispered, concerned when they couldn't detect any audible sounds coming from the room.

"Yeah, I'll be on my way in a little bit," she replied, trying to throw Damien off.

"Leave the phone on, alright?" Leslie said, just in case Damien tried to go too far.

"I know Brooke, I won't be long," Cindy said, feigning frustration. She could have easily been nominated for an Oscar with that performance. She pretended to push the end button on her phone, and placed it carefully inside her purse, speaker side up.

"Sorry, that was Brooke," Cindy said apologizing to Damien for her friend's interruption.

"That's okay; why is she rushing you?" he said.

"We have to leave early in the morning," she answered. "She has to be at work around noon."

"So you can't spend the night?" Damien asked, sounding sick and sincere at the same time.

"No, I can't spend the night, but I can stay for a little bit longer," she said.

Damien glanced at the clock that sat on the nightstand; it read 11:47.

*   *   *

"What's she saying, girl, what's she saying?" Stacey asked Leslie in a panic. Leslie's cell phone was planted on her cheek, and her eyes were in a trance.

"He's begging her to spend the night," Leslie whispered, frowning at Stacey and putting an index finger to her lips so Stacey would speak in a softer voice. Stacey drew nearer to Leslie's ear, in an effort to eavesdrop on the bootleg surveillance operation.

The wet, smacking sounds that invaded Leslie's ear let her know that Damien was pursuing Cindy's love in earnest.

Damien unlocked his lips from Cindy's, and moved his darting tongue across the front of her jasmine and sandalwood-scented neck. He slowly caressed Cindy's covered breasts with his warm hands, cupping and rubbing simultaneously. She reciprocated his intense excitement by kissing Damien on the neck, being careful not to suck too hard and leave a hicky. She used her hands to massage the sides of his head, rubbing his ears with her fingers in a sensual display of affection. Damien's sex organ pulsed with anticipation; he pulled the flimsy fabric of her skort up so he could palm her butt cheeks and engage in some heavy crotch grinding. He pulled her body against his, and snaked his hands inside the back of Cindy's skort, in an effort to expedite the foreplay process. Cindy's vagina was wet with desire, and her nipples hardened, causing them to stand firm against the fabric of her white tank top.

Damien started rotating his hips wildly, stabbing his bulging shorts against her crotch. He grabbed impatiently at her behind, squeezing and tugging with reckless abandon. *It's now or never,* Cindy thought, as she contemplated going all the way with Damien. She was really beginning to like him, but her senses told her different. Everything Leslie told her sounded genuine, and she didn't see any reason for her to lie. Plus, Damien's body language was beginning to show signs of desperation, a signal that he might be satisfied with just a one-night stand. Suddenly, she pushed Damien away, causing his eyes to widen with surprise. As Cindy's eyes filled with tears, a dreaded confession trickled from her lips.

"Stop... I can't."

"What do you mean, you can't?" Damien said, sounding like he was in shock.

"I...I thought I could, but I can't," Cindy said, as she began to tremble and sniffle simultaneously.

"What's wrong, Cindy?" Damien asked. He lifted his head, propping it up with his left arm, and wiped her tears with his free hand.

"I don't want to talk about it," Cindy said, leaving Damien stunned in amazement.

"C'mon Cindy, you can tell me, what's wrong?"

"I…I don't know, I…"

"C'mon baby, you can talk to me. It doesn't matter, just talk baby," Damien said, encouraging her to speak. Leslie handed the phone to Stacey, and snickered uncontrollably in her pillow. It was taking an incredible amount of self-control for her not to explode with laughter and give the prank away. She was delighted that Cindy decided to participate in her nasty trick. It was time for Damien to pay up.

"I broke up with my boyfriend six weeks ago," Cindy said. Damien's face twisted with concern, an expression that easily could have been confused with anger.

"And you're still upset?" Damien said sarcastically, rolling his eyes and raising the pitch of his voice. He was beginning to sound irritated, and Cindy could sense his impatience. It was time to diffuse him.

"It's not that…it's deeper than that, Damien."

"What? What happened?" Damien's eyebrows frowned, as his narrow pupils focused in on Cindy's well-tanned face.

"Damien, I had an abortion. He didn't want to get married or be a father."

"Damn," Damien said, sounding crushed.

"That's why we're down here," Cindy continued. "That's why Brooke is acting so protective over me. Plus, my body still doesn't feel right."

"So you thought teasing me would make you feel better?" Damien said. His erection had subsided, returning him to a normal state.

"No, Damien; actually, I really like you. I thought I could get over it by coming down here for the weekend, and when I met you, I was VERY interested. But when you started to grind on me, and I closed my eyes, I saw HIM." Cindy's doe-like eyes melted with salty tears that dripped silently down the side of her face. Her expression was convincing, and displayed a sincerity that belied her true feelings. Damien was stunned, and for the first time, speechless. He stared at Cindy for what seemed like an eternity, before breaking the uncomfortable silence.

"Cindy, you probably need to get going." Defeat rang from Damien's words. He sounded pitiful, as his voice whimpered through the night air. Leslie and Stacey gave each other high-fives, enjoying every minute of it.

"So that's it, just like that?" Cindy said, toying with Damien's emotions.

"No, it's not like that. I just have a sinking feeling in my heart, that's all," Damien said.

"I don't know if there's anything I can say or do that will make you feel better. And I apologize for rushing too… I had no idea—"

"Shhh," Cindy said, as she placed her index finger on his lip. "It's okay, it's not your fault. I told you, I still like you," she said, as she leaned forward to kiss Damien with her full, taut lips. They exchanged a quick smack, and sat up, one waiting for the other to break the uneasiness that filled the room.

"I'll walk you up," Damien said, as Cindy adjusted her top and bottom. Damien placed the top back on the box of chocolates, and straightened his clothes. Cindy reached over the foot of the bed for her purse, and quickly pushed the end button on her cell phone. She jangled her car keys to separate the door key from the others, and ran her fingers through her hair in an attempt to avoid a lengthy interrogation from Brooke. Damien opened the room door, and led the silent trek towards the stairs, with Cindy following. They ascended the stairwell, and walked across the darkness of the living area. Cindy's thong sandals slapped at the bottom of her heels, playing a lone note that echoed across the laminate flooring. Damien opened the door, walked onto the front porch, and paused, avoiding the sand and grass stains that awaited his socks.

"Call me," Damien said, as he gave Cindy a hug.

"I will," Cindy replied. She walked down the stairs, got into her car, and drove off. Damien watched as her taillights faded into the night, and let out a long, frustrating sigh. He walked back into the house, descended the stairwell, and disappeared into his room, feeling like a broken man.

*   *   *

Stacey and Leslie reveled in their satisfaction, and laughed about Damien's futile attempt to score until their stomach muscles twinged with pain. Stacey finally said goodnight to Leslie, and made her way upstairs to the room she shared with Kym.

Leslie lay silently on the bed, and watched the down rod and pull cord on the ceiling fan dance in unison. As she began to yawn and nod, she wondered if Cindy followed their plan to the letter. If so, Damien was in for another surprise. There was little doubt in her mind that after this night, Damien would think twice before trying to have his way with another woman.

*   *   *

18   Sunday Morning

Felicia's eyes fluttered slowly, as she adjusted to the sound of seagulls screeching and crying in the distance. It was Sunday morning, and she had pushed the snooze button on the digital alarm clock more than five times. She finally glanced at the numbers, which read 8:32. Normally, she would be up preparing breakfast, so she and Jordan could get a head start on the church crowd. She would be singing along with her favorite tunes on Praise 97.5, and waiting for *Bobby Jones Gospel* to come on TV. Today, she was waking up in unfamiliar territory, both literally and figuratively.

Her friendship with Antoine was in serious jeopardy; Kelvin's trust of her was questionable because of what she confided to Antoine about their marriage; and if word of the fight made it back to Concepts, she was going to have to shoulder the blame. She showered, dressed, woke Kelvin, and packed their belongings. She left the room to wake everyone else, except Antoine. He was already awake and dressed when Felicia walked downstairs. He glanced up from reading his Bible, made brief eye contact, and returned to his scriptures without saying a word. His travel bag was packed, and sitting next to his feet. Felicia assumed he didn't want to be bothered, and honored him with silence.

Damien woke up complaining about an upset stomach. By the time everyone got dressed and gathered their belongings, he had been to the bathroom twice, with a serious case of diarrhea. Leslie and Stacey snickered as they packed their belongings into the company car. They wondered how far Damien could drive with all of that Exlax running through his bowels. Leslie wanted to call Cindy and thank her personally, but she decided she would wait until they made it back to Atlanta.

Kelvin and Kym were the last ones to get dressed. After grabbing at the bagels and orange juice Felicia had put out on the kitchen counter, everyone loaded into their respective cars, and prepared to depart. As the two-vehicle caravan began its slow meander towards the island's exit, Felicia stared at the powdery sand dunes and homeless seagulls floating in the crisp morning breeze. Kym activated her cell phone, and connected to the Internet. Kelvin piloted the Expedition and surfed the local stations on the truck's radio. For the first time in almost three days, nothing was said. The cabin was mostly silent, except for some country music, morning gospel, and intermittent static while Kelvin's radio quietly scanned the airwaves.

The inside of the Taurus was just as silent. Antoine tuned the upbeat jazz selection that played softly out of his mind, and focused on the soft rays of sunlight that gleamed and danced playfully around the car's exterior. His thoughts were on his friendship with Felicia, and his fight with Kelvin. He couldn't believe that Felicia told Kelvin about Dontae, especially when he had sworn her to secrecy. He felt guilty for starting the fight with Kelvin, but everything happened so fast. He was ashamed, but proud; too proud to apologize or seek sympathy. He just wanted to make it back to Atlanta, straighten things out with Shauna, and get his life back on track, because at this point there definitely seemed to be more questions than answers.

Damien squirmed in his seat, as another rush of diarrhea invaded his bowels. He nearly lost his load, as the car veered onto the shoulder of the road near the bridge, and over a patch of rumble strips. As he corrected his steering, Stacey and Leslie grinned and snickered silently, purposely avoiding eye contact with each other. Stacey picked her *Essence* magazine back up and quickly found her mark, as Leslie stared out at the caramel colored waves as they rolled gently across the bay.

*   *   *

19 Monday Evening

Kym navigated and weaved her way through the bustling traffic on Peachtree Street. It was a little past seven-thirty, and the streets were still congested. As she drove past Lenox Mall towards Buckhead, she observed people from all walks of life engaged in a variety of activities. This was the part of Atlanta that most reminded her of home. She had been feeling homesick lately, and especially missed her family and friends. The warm climate, the swarm of cultures, Venice, Long Beach, all of the things that made So-Cal unique ran through her mind as her silver Acura melted into the sea of cars waiting for a green light.

As the sun descended towards the horizon, the nightlife on Peachtree began to spring to life. Young, energetic couples held hands as they crossed the busy intersection at Peachtree and Buckhead Avenue, and headed towards an assortment of hip, swanky happy-hour bars. Small groups of men dressed in hip-hop gear, and others in business casual attire conversed near the front of the ESPN Zone, hoping to intercept the sexy honeys that roamed about. Kym pushed on with the flow of traffic, as Hoobastank's song *Unaffected* blared through her CD player, drowning out the impatient drivers who blew their horns at slow pokes, flipping them off as they zoomed around into neighboring lanes.

She slowed as she approached a large, Spanish-styled restaurant on her right with an outdoor patio and white letters that spelled out The Cheesecake Factory above the open cluster of windows. She could see hostesses and servers bustling about as she turned into the restaurant's property. She stopped for a couple of pedestrians, and continued towards the valet parking lot.

She received her ticket, walked inside, and was welcomed by a young, handsome greeter. She told him that she was expecting a date, and he informed her that her date had already arrived. He led her past an array of busy servers and hungry patrons to a corner booth near the back of the restaurant, sat her down, and gave her a menu the size of a book to peruse. On the table lay a single red rose with a small card attached. She unfolded the card, and read it.

Hugs and Kisses.

P.S. I kept the cat clean for you.

Kym smiled as she inhaled the cool, sweet scent of the rose petals. She closed her eyes and fantasized about Valentine's Day, when she and her friend were lying naked in a bed full of rose petals, rubbing each other with oil, massaging each other slowly, caressing and probing, sharing each others sensuality, while candles flickered nearby, illuminating her bedroom with dancing shadows and a jasmine and sandalwood scent that carried them towards ecstasy. When she opened her eyes, Logan was standing in front of the booth smiling at her.

"Hey you," Kym said, as she placed the rose back on the table.

"Perfect timing," Logan replied.

She stood up and gave Logan a warm, sensual hug, caressing her back with her right hand. They sat down, ignoring a few unpleasant stares, and exchanged pleasantries while they waited for their server to take their order.

"Thanks for the rose," Kym said.

"I'm just glad you made it back. I was starting to miss you," Logan said.

Kym licked her lips slowly in a circular motion, as she analyzed the beauty of the woman she was sleeping with. If there was any reason Kym was staying in Atlanta, this was it. Studded diamond earrings highlighted Logan's close-cropped black hair. Her thin eyebrows arched perfectly over her dark brown eyes. Her symmetrical nose and slight lips gave away her Greek heritage. Her mouth displayed an almost perfect set of white teeth, which Kym loved to explore with her tongue. Logan's body was also well proportioned. At five-foot four and one hundred thirty-two pounds, they looked each other square in the eyes, unless one was wearing heels.

Logan complimented Kym on her choice of outfit, a crème pantsuit, and slid close enough to lock ankles with her most prized employee.

"How much did you miss me?" Kym asked.

"Maybe you can find out tonight," Logan said, as their server approached the table.

"Would you ladies care for a drink?" he asked, interrupting their lovers union.

"Water…I'll take water," Kym said.

"I'll take a glass of white wine," Logan said. "Your choice," she added, referring to the brand. Kym ordered the Caesar salad and a crab cake dinner, and Logan ordered the Thai chicken pasta.

"Kym, before we eat dinner, let me tell you that I was really impressed by the marketing plan that you guys put together. I must admit that I didn't know what to expect from this team building effort, but hopefully it's something we can capitalize on more often in the near future. I spoke with Steve over at the Bureau today; he will be coming over tomorrow to meet with me and review the proposal. He'll probably want to meet with you guys as well. Make sure your schedule is flexible and that everyone is in the office, okay?"

Kym's eyes shifted, and her smile disappeared from her face. Her demeanor suddenly changed; Logan could sense that something was up.

"Is everything okay?"

"Yeah."

"You sure?"

"I'm fine," Kym replied.

Logan eyed Kym and tried to read her facial expression, as the sounds of clanking silverware and the voices of strangers filled the air.

"So, did you make a decision?" Logan asked.

"Yeah."

"And?"

"It's me," Kym said, bringing her thin, oval-shaped eyes up to meet Logan's.

"Excuse me?"

"It's me," Kym said, repeating her statement. "I don't fit in with them," she said, as Logan looked on in disbelief.

"Kym, what are you talking about? Of course you fit in. That's why I chose you and Felicia to supervise this project. That's why I recommended you to manage the marketing research division. If it wasn't for you, we would have never pulled this off."

"Logan, I didn't do anything. Felicia ran the show. After what Leslie said to me, I was basically ineffective, and felt useless the entire time we were there."

"What? Said what, what did she say?" Logan was confused, and needed some answers. Her lover and lieutenant was experiencing clouded judgment. She told Kym before they left that one or more persons from her department was going to be laid off at the end of the quarter. Being that the deadline was only a month away, she felt that the Convention and Visitor's Bureau project would be a perfect time to find out who the weak link was. She left Kym in charge of making that decision; now she was wishing that she hadn't.

"She asked me about my racial background, said something about Affirmative-Action, asked me if I thought I was black or Korean, wanted to know what I checked on my financial aid, right in front of everybody."

Logan stared, wide-eyed and in shock, trying to absorb Kym's story. The server brought their drinks and Kym's salad, but Logan hardly noticed.

"Wait...Are you telling me that you were attacked because you are half-black?" Logan asked.

Kym exhaled sharply, and continued to explain her position. "That's not all, Logan. Other things happened that I'd rather not discuss, but the bottom line is, I just don't feel comfortable here anymore. I've been thinking about moving back to California...I don't know, I just don't know."

"Kym, are you crazy?" Logan said. "I have gone through hell to get you promoted through the ranks. You are in position to make well over six figures this year, and you're trying to throw it all away?"

"Exactly," Kym said.

"Exactly, what?" Logan said, desperately looking for a reply that made some sense.

"I've been promoted because we're lovers. I'm not effective as a leader. You would be wasting payroll dollars if you promoted me again. And if you leave me where I am, there's no way I would survive. I can't face them. Plus, Felicia did a much better job than I ever could have. That's who you need to thank. She's the one that put everything together. Give her the promotion, she deserves it."

Logan sat back in the booth and laid her head back on the leather seat. She was flattened by what she had just heard. She sighed deeply, and reached for her glass of wine. She ordered another, hoping it would make her drunk. In an instant, her job had become painfully difficult. Suddenly, she had some critical decisions to make. She was on the verge of losing her friend, her lover, and lieutenant. She twisted her fork nervously in her unfinished pasta dish, and contemplated her next move.

*   *   *

20   Friday, Two Weeks Later

The parking lot at Candies Gentlemen's Club was thick. Kelvin, Mack, and Damien climbed out of Kelvin's Ford Expedition, ready to see some hot action.

"C'mon dawg, I'm gonna show you how WE do it," Kelvin said. He and Mack were excited about officially indoctrinating Damien as a member of Atlanta's nightlife. They approached the front door, and slid in line behind two-dozen other men waiting to be frisked by the muscular bouncers. Damien studied the tan and lavender building, and black smoke mirrors that were used to keep Peeping Toms away from the action.

They were inside within ten minutes, exposing a whole new world to Damien. Most girls at the strip joints in Charlotte were young and dumb; the majority looked like they had just graduated from high school. These were not girls; these were definitely top-notch women. The décor of the club was different as well. Everything had a touch of class to it. The runways were extra clean, and orange mini-pendant lights hung above the private booths. Topless, bowtie-wearing bartenders served up the drinks, and the entertainers were dancing like true professionals. A sexy, honey-colored bartender seated them, and Kelvin ordered the first round of drinks. Damien excused himself and went to the restroom, as the emcee began introducing the night's second act.

"All right fellas, here we go! You need to get your money right for this one. Coming next to the stage, please put your hands together for Chyna!"

Red smoke poured from the dancer's entrance, as four girls on either side dressed in red and black leather cupless corsets, red four-inch heels, and crotchless panties writhed and wiggled to an instrumental version of R. Kelly's song "Thoia Thoing." Damien exited the bathroom just in time to see a sensual looking Amazon sister dressed like the others emerge through the thick, powdery smoke, only she wore a sheer cover-up and a red Zorro mask. The crowd near the stage began to swell, as men left their seats to get a closer look. Patrons began reaching into their pockets, unfolding knots of money to dole out to the hardworking dancers. As lights of rotating colors flashed off of Chyna's face, the crowd began to go wild.

"Take it off! Take it off!" they yelled. As she and her entourage moved towards center stage, one of the dancers pulled a short, red whip from the back of her neighbor's corset and handed it to Chyna. She let her hair down, revealing a long, wavy shoulder-length mane. She cracked the whip as she approached the hungry throng of spectators, grinding, twisting, and maneuvering her way down the line. Kelvin took his usual spot near the end of the stage and urged Damien to squeeze in, between him and Mack.

"I told you, Damien!" Kelvin said with excitement. Damien pulled some singles out of his pocket, and folded a couple of them long ways, so he could tease the dancers into coming closer. Chyna slowly approached the three, stopping to give them some personal attention. She turned around, jiggled her behind, ripped her cover-up off, and used it to wrap around the back of Kelvin's neck. When the mixed scents of anise, ginger, orange blossom, and amber floated through Kelvin's nose, he closed his eyes. Chyna bent down, pulled Kelvin close, and whispered into his ear.

"Cila qui rit vendredi va pleure dimanche."

Kelvin opened his eyes, stared at Chyna, and beamed from cheek to cheek. She gathered a few more tips, worked her way around the crowd, and sashayed back into the smoke, leaving Damien and Mack wondering what she said that left Kelvin in a trance.

*   *   *

Epilogue

Eve of the Annual Concepts Christmas Party

21 Thursday Evening

Damn, my baby looks stunning, Kelvin thought to himself. They had just valet parked, and were about to walk towards the shiny black, all-glass corporate building that housed Concepts Marketing, when a small, silver convertible BMW Z3 came zooming around the corner, and almost flattened the valet. Damien hopped out of the car, grabbed his black tuxedo coat off of the back seat, and ran around to the passenger's side door before the valet could reach it. He opened the door for his date, a dime-piece he had met at SciTrek during a networking mixture, and offered his hand to assist her in getting out.

"Damien Harris, look at you boy!" Kelvin exclaimed, as he dapped up his new homeboy.

"Look at me, look at YOU!" Damien said, eyeing Kelvin's tuxedo from head to toe. "No gators tonight?"

"Naw man, you know I had to get clean for my baby," Kelvin said, kissing Felicia on her cheek.

"Hello Damien," Felicia said, giving Damien a quick hug.

"Hey Felicia. I tell you, the way you look in that dress, with your hair all done up like that, smelling all good, Kelvin better watch out!" Damien said playfully.

"Yeah, yeah, whatever. Kelvin already told me on the way here that if I keep working out he's going to have to lock me up in the house," Felicia said, laughing.

"Damn right," Kelvin said.

"Aren't you going to introduce your date to us, Damien?" Felicia asked, as they made their way inside to escape the crisp winter breeze.

"I was getting to that...Felicia, Kelvin, this is Daniela. Daniela, this is Felicia, my new boss, and her husband Kelvin."

"Hello," Daniela said, as she extended her hand towards Felicia, and then Kelvin.

"Hi, you're such a pretty girl," Felicia said.

"Thank you," Daniela said. Her accent and meek demeanor was a dead giveaway that she wasn't from the United States. She had dark, shoulder-length hair, thick eyebrows, piercing hazel eyes, and a pearl-white smile. She stood about 5'8 in her heels, and her skin was the color of golden cappuccino; she looked to be fresh out of college.

"Felicia, why don't you and Daniela go ahead and check your coats in while Kelvin and I hit the men's room for a second," Damien said.

"There you go," Felicia said, as she and Daniela turned to walk towards the coat check-in desk. Felicia's hair was pinned up, and her diamond chandelier earrings glittered under the lobby's bright lights. Kelvin did a double take, still in awe of Felicia's stunning looks. He and Damien went into the lobby bathroom to relieve themselves before heading up towards the party.

"Boy, it looks like you got yourself a winner," Kelvin said, as he tinkled into the urinal.

"Ahh, you know how it goes," Damien replied. "I always keeps me some backup. She might work out, and she might not. Her daddy is some kind of Ambassador from Brazil or something. He sent her to Oglethorpe to try and shelter her, but you know a brotha as smooth as me had to put that irresistible conversation on ole girl." Damien finished up and headed towards the sink.

"You spoke to Mack today?" Damien asked.

"Yeah, he and Stacey oughta be here any minute," Kelvin replied.

"Sheeit, I knew that nigga was sprung the night you recognized her at Candies," Damien said.

"Yeah, you know how it goes. If I can't get it, it's only right my homeboy can. Hell, I can't even get that nigga to go out no more; she must be puttin' it on his ass," Kelvin said, laughing as he dried his hands under the dryer. They walked back into the lobby to find Felicia and Daniela conversating with a small group of co-workers. They spoke, and then ushered them towards the elevators. As they neared the twenty-eighth floor, the sounds of a jazz trio playing "Chestnuts on an Open Fire" floated into the elevator.

They walked into a large conference room that was beautifully decorated for the occasion, and found their reserved seats. The large glass windowpane allowed the guests to overlook the sleek, sophisticated skyline of the Atlanta perimeter. Marketing executives, clients, junior associates, assistants, and their dates mingled over champagne, spiked eggnog, and hors d'oeuvres. Damien and Kelvin headed towards the open bar, while Logan found Felicia sitting with Daniela at their table.

"Hey Felicia," Logan said. "You look great!"

"Why thank you, Logan."

"Who is your friend?"

"Oh, she's with Damien," Felicia said.

"Hi friend, I'm Logan." She extended a courteous handshake to Daniela.

"Nice to meet you, I'm Daniela," she replied with a smile.

"Have a seat Logan," Felicia said.

"No, that's okay; I've got to make my rounds with the clients. Felicia, I just wanted to let you know that you're doing an excellent job in your new position. I wanted to be the first person to tell you that."

"Thanks, Logan. It's going to look real good on my resume when I finish my MBA program this summer," Felicia said.

"You're not leaving us too, are you?" Logan said. "I already lost Kym, and Antoine resigned last month."

"Wherever the good Lord leads me, that's where I'll be," Felicia said.

"I'd sure hate to lose you Felicia, but you know you would leave HIGHLY recommended."

"Thanks, I appreciate that," Felicia replied.

Logan excused herself, as Daniela and Felicia awaited Damien and Kelvin's return. Felicia sat silently, brimming with confidence as she tapped her fingers to the sounds of the live band. She wondered if Antoine was happy with his new wife, new job in Miami, and child-to-be, and how Kym was holding up in California. Leslie had asked for, and received a transfer out of Logan's department for personal reasons. The rumor mill said that it had something to do with their trip to St. George, but Felicia hadn't bothered to ask.

It had been a wild year at Concepts, and Felicia was glad to see it coming to a close. The lights and ornaments on the huge Christmas tree emitted colorful hues that glittered and sparkled in the dimly lit room. The fire from the red and white table candles danced in unison, as the waiters prepared to serve the hungry guests. She looked across the room at Kelvin and Damien, and cracked a smile. *Look at them,* she thought to herself. *They look like two kids on a playground. Yeah, two big, inseparable kids. But I love my man. And now, I love my life...yeah, that's it. I really, really, love my life. And right about now, I wouldn't trade it for anything in the world...*

Meet the Author

Kenny Blue is the newest author on the African-American literary scene. According to Kenny, his goal is to "entertain a diverse readership by telling compelling, entertaining, and powerful stories of fiction based upon issues facing African-Americans today." According to Kenny, he found his love of writing by accident. As a child, he remembers reading several popular novels, including the classic *Jaws* by Peter Benchley. He also perused many of the science-fiction paperbacks that his dad collected from Goodwill. An avid daydreamer, Kenny remembers being chastised by many of his teachers for "not paying attention." His excuse is that his imagination was working in overdrive. In college, Kenny became a history buff, and changed his major from Civil Engineering to African-American Studies. He went on to earn his master's degree in Secondary Education, and became a teacher in the public school system. Yearning to explore his writing and research talents, Kenny prayed for eight months straight during the year 2003 for God to show him favor and direction. In April, Kenny's prayers were answered. He awoke one morning with a vision that would alter his life's path forever. The title of a book, *The Beach House*, as well as a storyline, was embedded into his conscience. From that day forward, Kenny considered himself an author. *The Beach House* is Kenny Blue's debut novel, and as he describes, "my first steps into the light." Kenny lives near the Atlanta suburb of Lithonia with his wife and daughter. His hobbies include traveling, reading, grilling, and playing basketball.

Kenny Blue can be contacted through his web site,
www.kennyblue.com.